~Before I Lay Me Down to Sleep~

"An Urban Fiction Romance"

"The thing that is worse than death is betrayal."~ Malcolm X

~Gail~

"What in the world is taking Dr. Erickson so long?" Gail wondered aloud.

Anxiously bouncing her right leg, she glances down at her wrist watch for the tenth time.

She's been nervous ever since receiving a phone call from her gynecologist nurse Veronica.

Veronica stated that her test results were in and for Gail and her husband to come into the office immediately. The request from Dr. Erickson to have Chaz come along is what's concerning her the most.

"Lord please, if this man has given me another STD I will become one of the newest movies playing on the lifetime channel... burning bed... the sequel."

"Gail who are you talking to?" a familiar voice asked.

Gail spun around to see Dr. Erickson leaning against his office door with her chart in hand.

"Oh hey Dr. Erickson, I wasn't talking to anyone, I was just thinking aloud. You know me, always thinking about something." A nervous laugh escaped her mouth.

"Now Gail we've talked about this, call me Ollie. You helped me through a rough period in my life. You're not only my patient, but you are my friend. I couldn't have gotten through my divorce without you." said Dr. Erickson.

"Oh Ollie, I was just doing my job. I'm a Psychologist, that's what we do; we're healers, as my grandmother would say."

"And a healer you are. You helped me to forgive my ex-wife and to let go. All of the talks we had, exercises and books that you recommended really aided in healing my broken heart. Now look at me; my private practice is doing amazing, my self-esteem is through the roof, and the ladies love me! And I have you to thank."

"Not at all Ollie, you can thank God; I just helped out a bit."

They both laughed simultaneously.

Gail leans back in her chair and speaks softly.

"You've found something wrong with me haven't you? There's a reason you wanted Chaz to come with me to receive the results."

"Where is he?" Dr. Erickson asked.

"Obviously not here so what is it already?" Gail impatiently replied.

"Your pap smear came back abnormal. We explained that most the time abnormal cell changes on the cervix are caused by human papillomavirus, which is a sexually transmitted disease. This prompted us to do a colposcopy or cervical biopsy to run test on the abnormal cells."

"Right and you told me that usually the abnormal cells will go away on their own." stated Gail.

"Yes but I also said that it depended on what type of HPV we were dealing with. You haven't had a pap smear in 10 years prior to this one." Explained Dr. Erickson.

"It slipped my mind," she shamefully replied.

"Yes, you informed me of that. With the symptoms you've been having; the abnormal vaginal bleeding after intercourse, the fatigue, the longer heavier periods, and the pelvic and back pain; Gail I don't know any other way to say this but to say it."

Dr. Erickson looks at his friend with the saddest eyes and continues.

"The biopsy results report that you have cervical cancer. You will undergo further test to determine whether the cancer has spread and to what extent; this process is called 'staging'. The stage of the cancer is a key factor in deciding on treatment. It seems like we need to run test as soon as possible."

He walks over to her and put his hand on her shoulder.

"Gail, are you listening to me? We need to start testing immediately so we can see which treatment we need to begin."

She sat there staring at the wall behind him with tears lining her face.

"Gail I'm sorr..."

She reaches out to hug him.

"It's okay Ollie. I'm free after four pm all next week. Have Veronica give me a call with available days and times."

"Are you going to be alright Gail?"

Breaking their embrace, she walks to his office door.

"I will be" she said over her shoulder. The walk to her car seemed like it took forever. Shaking and crying uncontrollably, she was in no shape to drive, so she grabbed her cell phone and dialed her husband's number. Ringing only once, she was sent straight to the voicemail.

"Um, hey Honey, I waited for you at Dr. Erickson's office, but you never showed up; guess you were busy. Any who, the news wasn't so great, I'm a complete wreck, I've been sitting in the car crying and wondering why is this happening to me."

She let out a long sigh before continuing.

"Well Honey, I'm going to head on home and get some rest. After a good nap I'll start on dinner, I love you, bye."

She loves music, but she can't handle any extra activity at the moment, so she decides to drive home in silence.

How could this be happening to me? I mean, I eat right, exercise, pray, tithe, volunteer at women shelters and children hospitals. I've never killed, beat up, scammed, or flat out harmed anybody in my entire life and yet I'm stricken with cancer. This is not fair; why Jesus?

As she pulls up to her home, she notices her husband's car parked in their drive way.

Hmm, I didn't expect him to be home so early, she thought.

Upon entering their home, she hears a familiar song playing softly in their bedroom.

"Aw, he must have heard my voicemail and decided to play our favorite song. He knows Janet Jackson always cheers me up."

She sings along with the lyrics as she climbs the stairs to their bedroom.

"Anytime, and any place, I don't care who's around..."

She stops singing when she hears moaning on the other side of the door.

Turning the door knob slowly, she stands outside of the room in complete and utter shock; her husband is getting head from someone submerged under their bed covers. Quietly closing the door, she heads downstairs to her office.

"This bastard just can't stop cheating can he?" she mutters while opening the safe hidden under her desk. She retrieves the .22 her father gave her before she was married for protection, because she lived alone. Loaded and ready, all she had to do was take the safety off and shoot.

Gail crept slowly back up to the bedroom; she stands outside of the door re-thinking her actions. Just as she decides that it isn't worth going to jail for she hears, "Oooooo Monroe, you're about to make me cum." Covering her mouth, she speaks through the spaces between her fingers.

"Monroe? It can't be."

Enraged she burst into the bedroom and points the gun at her husband.

"Gail! Oh my gosh! What are you doing here?! Baby it's not what it looks like."

"Bastard I live here, that's what I'm doing here and it's EXACTLY what it looks like."

Her aim switches from her husband to the covers.

"Monroe come from under the covers and reveal your backstabbing, trifling face. My own brother caught giving fallacio to my husband...how could you?"

Emerging from under the covers with a sinister smile, Monroe lays his head on Chaz's chest.

"Well how couldn't I? He is just too sexy! Gail I'm sorry, but I had to give him a real orgasm because from what he tells me, he's been faking it for a long time now. Plus I grew tired of wondering how he tasted... so here we are."

Monroe flips the covers to the side disclosing him and Chaz nakedness. He walks over to the dresser and pauses the iPod playing before slipping on his t-shirt and shorts; sitting on the edge of bed he puts on his shoes and gazes up at his sister.

"Gail, chile, put that gun away. All three of us know that you won't hurt a fly, and besides, how would it look if the beautiful thirty seven year old Gail Washington, owner and founder of "The Healing Center," a member of the Distinguished American Psychological Association, an avid volunteer in her community and the best damn psychologist in all of Chicago land, shoot her homosexual younger brother for sleeping with her cheating no good husband? Darling all that you've worked for will be shot to hell. Your life will be ruined, so put the gun away and get a divorce. " he says.

She slowly lowers the gun as he pushes past her to exit the room. Half way down the stairs Monroe looks back at his lover and sister to further taunt her.

"Oh and Honey, he taste delicious!"

Feeling betrayed and sick by the entire situation, Gail had heard enough. She stands there letting her brother's last statement marinate and before she knows it, she runs down the stairs and takes three shots at Monroe as he pulls off in a car that has to belong to one of his newest boyfriends because he doesn't own one. She cracks the windshield with one shot and put two in the hood.

"I better not ever see you again Monroe! NOT EVER!"

She scoops up the shells and storms back into the house screaming Chaz's name.

"Chaz bring your wretched sweet booty ass out here! You hear me calling you!"

Sprinting up the stairs to the bedroom she tries to enter but can't, Chaz has locked himself inside.

"Chaz open this damn door!"

"HELL NO! YOU'RE CRAZY RIGHT NOW! WHAT IS WRONG WITH YOU?!" he yelled.

Frustrated by his stupid question, Gail kicks the door.

"What's wrong with me?! What's wrong with me?! I have a husband who thinks his penis is a tampon! He just sticks it in whoever has a hole! He gave me chlamydia and HPV! And now after finding out I have cervical cancer, I find him once again sharing our bed with someone else; but this time he's sharing our bed with my younger brother!"

She takes a few steps back and aims at the door.

"Chaz you have five seconds to open this door or else I will shoot it down... and then shoot you down... ONE!"

Before she finishes saying two, Chaz is unlocking the door. He walks up to her like a child who knows they are in major trouble.

"You have cervical cancer? Honey for how long?"

He tries to embrace his wife, but she backs away.

"Don't act so concerned now. You didn't care enough to come to the doctor's office and receive this horrible news with me, so why ask for details? I want you to get your things and get out. I don't care where you go or how you get there, but you won't be staying in my house or driving the car that I bought."

"But Gail where am I sup..."

"I JUST SAID THAT I DON'T GIVE A DAMN! Now get the hell out before I empty this gun between your legs!"

That last threat is all that it took for Chaz to start scrambling to gather as many things as he could. Gail watches him scurry around their bedroom, like a cockroach when the lights are cut on.

"Okay, I think you've packed enough, leave before I change my mind about allowing you to leave on your own two feet and not on a stretcher." she warns him. "Why Chaz why? I'm not pretty enough for you? How come you never told me that you weren't satisfied with our love life? How come you never manned up and said that I just wasn't good enough for you?" she asks as she caught a glimpse of herself in the mirror.

"Gail look at you; you are gorgeous! Flawless chocolate skin, piercing gray eyes, long beautiful legs and ass you can bounce a quarter off of. You cook, you clean, you wash, you do your best to take care of me, but sometimes things aren't what they seem. I tried to be a man... a good husband to you but I can't and I have my reasons. One day maybe you'll find it in your heart to let me explain..."

"Please, save it. There's nothing you can tell me to make me turn the other cheek; not this time buddy. You can just get the hell out!"

She waits until he makes it to the end of the walk way before suggesting for his own good to never return. Gail watches her husband of five years as his image fades into the distance. The sirens of squad cars speeding down her block snatches her attention.

Well it took them long enough; I could've killed both of them and been across the border by now. I know Mrs. Kennedy nosy tail is the one that called them.

She quickly tosses the gun into the bushes and waits for the officers to approach her.

"Ma'am it was reported that screams and gun shots were heard coming from this home, do you live here?" asked the officer.

"Yes I do and yes there were screams and gun shots, but it came from the television;

I was watching CSI: Miami. My crush Horatio was shot and I screamed. I'm sorry for all of the trouble I've caused."

Unconvinced, the initial officer looked back at his partner.

"Ma'am, do you mind if we take a look around?"

"Sure you can if you provide me with a warrant," replied Gail.

"Man let's go. If she says she's good, then she's good." said the other officer.

"You take care ma'am, and try not to get so worked up over a TV show and what not."

"I'll keep that in mind officer, have a good day."

Gail gazes at the officers as they hop into their squad car and speed off. She looks over at Mrs. Kennedy's house and spots her peeking through her blinds. Gail just shakes her head at her nosy neighbor before retrieving the gun out of the bushes.

She secures her pistol in the safe and quickly decides she needs to close her eyes for a few hours before she finds herself doing something else crazy. By the time she makes it to the bedroom; the tears were falling nonstop.

Kneeling at the edge of her bed, she begins to pray.

"Lord, please help me. I don't know what to do. Please tell me what to do. I don't know what to do..."

"Gail?"

Her eyes pop open when she hears her secretary's voice.

"Zaya what are you doing here?" asked Gail.

"When you didn't show up at the office after your appointment, I knew something was wrong. I've been calling and texting you, but you haven't responded. Gail you never stand up your patients and you always answer your phone; I had to come over." answered Zaya.

Pulling herself up from the floor, she looks Zaya in the eyes.

"I thought I made it clear that the spare key I gave you was only to be used in case of an emergency." said Gail.

"It is an emergency, I was worried about my good friend, so I came to check on her."

"Zaya please leave, I don't want you to see me like this."

"See you like what Gail?" inquired Zaya.

"Like this! Pitiful! I'm so pitiful Zaya!"

Gail collapses onto the floor.

Alarmed by her friend's emotional outburst, Zaya drops to her knees and wraps her arms around Gail.

"Gail what is going on? Talk to me."

"Do you really want to know?"

"Yes, of course." replied Zaya.

"Okay, well um, Dr. Erickson says that I have cervical cancer and I should come back for more tests to see what stage its in. I leave there and immediately phone Chaz to tell him about this disheartening news, only to come home and find his penis in my little brother's mouth."

"Oh my gosh Gail! What in the world?! I am so sorry! You will get through all of this. We will pray you through this. The devil is a liar! Lord what is wrong with Monroe?!"

Gail's sobs cause Zaya to shed some tears of her own, but she knows that she has to pull herself together and be of some support to Gail. Re-assuring Gail that everything will be alright, she tightens her arms around her friend and holds her as if she's shielding her from her painful reality.

"Gail, look at me, I need you to go into the guest bedroom and get some sleep. I will clean up in here, and then go to the office and cancel all of your appointments for the rest of the week. I will call and stop by periodically until you feel better. No clients, no paperwork, no nosy neighbors and friends... as a matter of fact, turn off your work cell phone. I don't want you to do anything mentally or physically strenuous; just rest as much as possible... you hear me?"

Too exhausted to respond, Gail gives a slight nod and makes her way to the guest bedroom. Keeping her word, Zaya begin cleaning up the evidence of Chaz's affair, which sparks memories of her own past relationship. It was only two years ago she was a night away from being a married woman. That was until she thought it would be a fun idea to crash her fiancé's bachelor party thrown the night before the wedding. The bridesmaids tried to warn her not to go, but she went anyway and she was glad that she did. When her fiancé's best friend Jake opened the door to his condo and seen her, he turned white as a ghost. He tried to deny her entry, but she forced her way inside. She didn't see him in the living area with everyone else so her gut told her to check the bedroom. Once again Jake tried to stop her, but she twisted his ear until he moved from in front of the door. When she walked in, there was the man she was about to spend the rest of her life with, having sex with one of the hired strippers. She grabbed some rubbing alcohol from the dresser, reached inside her purse and walked towards the bed...

Ever since that night all men were nothing but dogs and not worth her time or effort. Pushing that memory to the back of her mind, she got back to work. After cleaning and making some homemade chicken noodle soup, she left a note on the night stand where Gail was resting stating that she is going to the office to cancel this week's appointments and that she will call her in the morning. Pulling the covers over her friend, Zaya reassured Gail once more that things will be alright.

Gail pretended to be asleep until she heard Zaya leave. The events of the day were causing her to seriously re-evaluate her life.

"Monroe is right. If I would've shot them both all of my accolades, achievements, and hard work would've went down the drain, and that is not an option. I need to pull myself together and push through this. I've busted my butt to attain my doctorate and make a name for myself and no man or disease can take that away from me. Yes, I have cancer but it may be in the beginning stages and able to be stopped. With prayer and following the doctor's orders, I should be fine. As for Chaz, he'll be served with divorce papers real soon." Gail said aloud.

She grabs her cell phone and dialed Zaya's number.

"Gail I thought you were sleeping."

"Never mind that; I would like for you to call Dr. Erickson's office first thing in the morning and schedule me an appointment."

"Okay got it, anything else?"

"Yes reschedule all of the cancelled appointments for next week, I should be ready to come back by then."

"Gail, are you sure because…"

"Zaya I'm sure; I'll talk to you soon. Have a good night."

"Hey I'm worried about you. You know I'll be over there every day all up in your face."

"Yes I know, bye." Gail said laughingly.

"It's not bye, it's see you later." said Zaya.

"Okay, see you later, now get off my line crazy girl."

Immediately after hanging up with Zaya, she calls her father, a well-established intellectual property lawyer to ask for a favor.

"Hi dad, how are you? Yes, that's great, hey I need a huge favor; you wouldn't know any really good divorce attorneys would you?"

"Whew wee I'm tired! I don't want to hear a damn thing from another person tonight. I'm locking up this office and carrying my tail home," said Zaya as she locked the final door to the building. She thanked God that she only parked two buildings down from the Healing Center because she was exhausted. On her way to her car she heard a man and woman arguing across the street.

"You pompous egotistical jerk! I can't believe that I agreed to go out with you!" she shouted.

"Oh we both know why you agreed to go on a date with me. I'm one of the top pediatric surgeons in Illinois and I'm undeniably handsome. You should be grateful that someone of my stature even approached you... not to mention be seen in public with you. You're a basic broad who's a waitress for

God's sake. You can't even afford an idea let alone a new pair of shoes." He retorted.

"No this mutha sucka didn't!" blurted Zaya.

Before he knew it, the woman smacks him, and then storms off.

"THAT'S OKAY YOU'LL BE BACK! THEY ALWAYS WANT TO COME BACK AFTER THEY REALIZE IT'S NOT A LOT OF MEN LIKE ME TO CHOOSE FROM!" he yelled.

"Hell I hope not!" said Zaya

Zaya watched the man try to mac another woman strolling down the street like he didn't just get played.

Zaya shakes her head hops in her car and drives off, "Men ain't shit!"

"Beauty and the devil are the same thing."~ Robert Mapplethorpe

~Nathaniel~

"Like I previously explained; an anesthesiologist will give Olivia general anesthesia which will relax her muscles and induce sleep. The procedure will begin by making a small incision, about two to three centimeters at the base of the belly button. I will then identify the hernia sac containing the bulging intestine. I will push the intestine back into its proper place behind the muscle wall and then remove the sac. The muscle wall will be reinforced with multiple layers of stitches to prevent another hernia. I will then sew the skin around the belly button down to the underlying muscle so it will look like an innie instead of an outie. After that, a bulky pressure dressing will be applied over the incision to provide support to the repaired muscle and tissue. The entire procedure should take no more than one hour. I've done umbilical hernia surgeries before Mr. & Mrs. Korver, all successful, so I know Olivia will be just fine."

He gives Olivia a wink and calls in the Anesthesiologist.

"Okay Olivia remember what I told you, there's nothing to be afraid of. My friend Dr. Lynn is going to give you some medicine through this tube here that's going to make you sleepy Okay? When you wake up, that lump behind your belly button will be gone." explains Nathaniel

"It will be gone like magic?!" asked Olivia

"Yep, just like magic."

"No more tummy aches?!"

"Nope, no more tummy aches; unless you eat lots and lots of ice cream!"

"Ooooooooo I love ice cream Dr. Thompson!" Olivia shouted

Nathaniel looked down at Olivia's sweet face as she lays down on the gurney and gives her a little flick under the chin making her giggle.

"I do too kiddo"

"Alright sweetie, here's Dr. Lynn, you're going to feel a little pinch from the IV as she inserts it into your arm, but try to relax as much as you can. You think you can do that?"

"Ugh, I hate shots but I'll be still," said Olivia.

"You'll be fine honey, daddy and I will be right here when you wake up, ready to take you home," Said Mrs. Korver.

"Okay mom, Dr. Lynn I'm ready."

Everyone burst into laughter.

"Wow, you're a big girl aren't you? Alright, here we go, take a deep breath and count to twenty with me... one..."

Dr. Lynn continues to count slowly and before she makes it to fourteen, Olivia is fast asleep.

The surgery goes smoothly, which is the norm for Dr. Thompson; he is one of the top pediatric surgeons in the country. 'Another job well done' is what he hears from a few of his peers as he heads to the locker room for a shower. Today is Wednesday, and every Wednesday he has lunch with his dad. He adores his father; they are as thick as thieves. Ever since he was a little boy, he and his father developed this bond that nothing or no one could ever break. Whatever he wanted to do in life, his father was behind him one hundred percent. His mother on the other hand... not so much. He strips down and turns on the shower. He leans into the hot water and grimaces as he runs his fingers across a large

'R' shaped keloid scar on the lower left side of his back. He holds his breath to try and push the horrid memory out of his mind, but like a freight train, the pain rushes him, forcing him to lean against the shower wall for support.

He was laying on the floor in his bedroom playing with his toy race cars when she came in twirling her hair and smoking a Newport.

"Boy, look at you; you think that you're all of that because you have hazel eyes and dimples; well let me tell you something, you're ugly! Always have been and always will be! You and your father walk around here like you are God's gift to women and that is far from the truth! Both of you do nothing but make my life miserable! I wish I never had you, I wanted a little girl anyway!"

She spoke with disgust in her voice and hate in her eyes. She used his wall to put out her cigarette and then flicked the bud in his direction.

"But mama, what did I do? Why are you so mad at me?"

He wished he'd never said that because, she snatched him up by the arm and smacked him down again.

"How many times must I tell you to stop calling me mama? It's Rachel to you! Since you can't seem to get it through your thick skull let me help you to remember."

She turned him onto his stomach and held him down.

"This will teach you to do as I tell you." She said as she removed a pocket knife from her knee high boots. She lifted up his shirt and began to carve her name into his back. It was like pain he'd never felt before. He remembered begging for her to stop; that he'll remember to call her Rachel from then on out.

"RACHEL!!!! YOUR NAME IS RACHEL!!!! NOT MAMA!!!!" He screamed in agony

She wiped the blood off her knife onto his pants and stood over him.

"If you call me mama again, I'll carve the rest of my name on your face making you uglier than you already are; and I will not stop no matter how much you scream, understood?"

All he remembers is saying, 'Yes', before falling asleep. He was about six years old.

Nathaniel gasps and covers his mouth as if appalled by his own dreadful flashback. He hadn't realized how long he was in the shower, until he glances at the clock on the locker room wall seeing that it was three thirty-five; which only gives him twenty-five minutes to make it to downtown Chicago to meet his father for lunch.

Nathaniel Thompson is a tall brown skin man with hazel eyes and two deep dimples. He sports a low fade and he has the build of a NBA power forward. He slides into a nice pair of grey slacks, with a crisp white collared shirt, a grey tie and vest, with a pair of white Gucci loafers. He checks himself over in the mirror inside his locker once more before heading out. He smiles at how handsome he is, but smiling isn't able to hide the sadness in his eyes from remembering that horrible day.

"Pull yourself together Nathaniel; that was twenty-five years ago, get over it. You're intelligent, you're successful, and despite what Rachel thinks, you're not ugly. She was wrong, you are God's gift to women; every woman on this planet wants you to wife them. She was just mad because poppa was a rolling stone. She wasn't good enough to be his wife or any other man's wife."

Shaking off the ill feelings, he grabs his keys and heads out the locker room.

Traffic was better than he expected; he made it downtown on time to his dad's favorite restaurant; Lawry's on east Ontario Street.

"Good afternoon Mr. Thompson, your father is waiting for you."

"Good afternoon Sherri, is he at our usual table?"

"Well of course sir. He's already ordered for the both of you, so your meal should be up promptly."

Nathaniel says thank you over his shoulder and heads to the back of the restaurant to a table tucked away in the left hand corner.

Just as he's about to greet his father with his usual, "Hey Pops, what's happening!" he notices something different about him.

He looks old and drained. His eyes are low and his hands are trembling as he turns the pages of the drink menu. He looks worried; almost troubled by something.

"What's going on Pops?"

"Hey son, I thought you had stood me up for a minute. Did your last procedure run longer than expected?"

"Oh no, it went smoothly, there was an accident on the expressway, so it was backed up pretty bad."

God, I hate lying to him. But I can't tell him that I was late because I was reminiscing about my dreadful childhood

"Dad, it seems like there is something troubling you; what is it?"

His dad nervously grabs his glass of water and takes a sip.

"I've been keeping something from you for years now, and I think it's about time that I came clean."

Shifting in his seat; Nathaniel became nervous as well.

"Son, the nursing home called me and said that Rachel doesn't have too much time left. Her Alzheimer's has gotten worse; she no longer can carry on a conversation or respond to her environment. I want you to go see your mother and make peace with her; it's important to me that you do this son."

"Wait a minute, how do you know she's in a nursing home and the status of her health? You've been seeing her behind my back? How could you, when you know of all the despicable things she's done to me?" questioned Nathaniel

"I knew you would feel this way, that's why I haven't mentioned it to you. I've been seeing her at Lakeshore Rehabilitation Center for about four years now. One of my old friends from high school works there and he called me up on the day she was admitted. I thought to myself, here's my chance to right some wrongs, here's my chance to apologize and ask for forgiveness for all that I put her through. Son, I feel responsible for the things she did to you. I feel like it's my fault for her hurting you. If I would have been a better man to her, maybe she would have been a better mother to our son. I believe she took her anger for me out on you and for that I'm deeply regretful."

"Dad what she did to me have nothing to do with you and you know that. She was just an evil, bitter woman that couldn't stand on her own two. She always looked for the easy way instead of working hard like a normal person to get the things she wanted in life. Yes, you weren't on your best behavior back in the day, but that is no excuse for the things she subjected me to. So don't you go blaming yourself for what her crazy ass has done; you hear me dad, what happened is not your fault."

"Nathaniel listen to me; she doesn't remember any of it. She doesn't even remember who I am. When I found out she had Alzheimer's, I knew I had a clean slate. I knew I had an opportunity to be the man to her that I should've been years ago. Every Tuesday and Thursday I go visit her and we read, look at pictures, listen to music, in hopes that doing these things will trigger her memory, but..."

"Look dad, I came here to eat and chat with you, and not talk about someone I could care less about. I'm all done with this conversation; let's talk about something else."

"Not until you say that you're going to visit her before she passes; which is any day now."

Irritated Nathaniel tosses his napkin onto the table.

"Dad for what reason? I'm good; scouts honor."

"For what? Son you don't respect women at all. You treat them like that napkin right there; you use them and then throw them away. You consider them beneath you and only worth one thing; a good time. I don't want you to live like this anymore. I want a wife for you. I want grandchildren Nate. You know if I could be honest here; I always wondered how someone could be as beautiful as your mother but possess such evilness inside; and now I'm starting to wonder the same about you. Son you have to stop treating women the way that you do. It's just not right."

Nathaniel is taken aback by his father in a way, because he was comparing him to his mother, Rachel.

"So you think talking to Rachel is going to make me respect women? Don't you think it's only going to make me despise them even more?"

The words came out of his mouth before he had a chance to catch them.

Why did I just say that? Is this how I really feel about women?

"No not just that. I believe it would also help if you talked to Dr. Washington. She's an excellent therapist; the best in Chicago."

This old man must be off his rocker. He wants me to talk to the devil and a shrink? Oh hell no!

"So let me get this straight; you want me to see a shrink so she could aid me in forgiving Rachel?"

"Yes! Please son, before I go, I would love to see you in love; happy for once in your damn life. Yes, you're rich and handsome, I mean the latter you get from your father, but that shouldn't be enough. Don't you want the white picket fence, with the dog, kids and beautiful wife? Huh, don't you? Son I know you do. You can't possibly be satisfied with your love life right now, are you?" asked his father.

"Dad I'm perfectly fine. I told you I had a date the other night and what do you mean before you go?"

"Yea and she ended it by smacking the hell out of you. You deserved it. You said some pretty foul things to her. I meant I'm getting old, so calm down."

He reaches across the table and places a business card in his son's hand.

"Please Nate, I'm begging you, go see Dr. Washington. She's great, she helped me to overcome some childhood demons of my own and for that I am grateful. If it wasn't for her, I wouldn't have ever made peace with my past or with your mother. I'm telling you son, you won't regret it."

Nathaniel nods yes just as the waitress approaches with their entrée's. Both men nod and say thank you to the waitress before returning to their conversation. Nathaniel flips the card over and reads it.

Gail Washington, PH.D.

The Healing Center

Psychotherapy for adults, adolescents & couples

T: 312.745.9160

F: 312.745.9161

1030 N. Lakeshore Drive, Chicago, IL 60611

He stuffs the card into his vest pocket and sparks up a lighter conversation with this father. They laugh, eat and have a couple of glasses of wine. Everything returns back to normal. It's like any other lunch meeting they've had. He says his goodbyes to his dad and hit the highway to his townhouse. He's never broken a promise so he makes it up in his mind to give Dr. Washington a call after a well needed nap.

He turns into the alley and presses his garage door remote; he whips in but stops abruptly.

"Oh shit! What the hell?"

A five foot five, brown haired, curvy woman with a bat in her hands is posted up against the wall; and she looks angry.

"Cara, what the hell are you doing in my garage? How did you even get in here?"

"Don't worry about that. How come you haven't been returning my calls Nate? I know it's someone else; who is she?"

"Cara I don't owe you any explanations. I'm single. We had sex a few times that's not even worth remembering, so please stop the madness and get the hell out."

"Excuse me? My sex is top notch and you know it! I thought we had something special Nate!"

"Well you thought wrong. I mean think about it; what can you offer me? You're a nanny; you sing the alphabet all day and change diapers. What kind of money does a job like that bring in annually? Not only can't your bank account compete with mines, your bedroom skills are whack as hell. You were out like a light after the first round AND you don't know how to give decent head. Cara please, I'm a grown man that doesn't have time for worthless broads like you. Now this is the last time I'm going to ask; get... out... of... my... garage." Cara raises the bat over her head and stares at him with fire in her eyes.

"You know what? Fuck you Nate!"

She swings the bat knocking off the side mirror. He sprints towards her, but she goes to the other side of the car.

"Chick have you lost your ever loving mind?!"

She answers by busting out his right back window and then bolting out of the garage. He ran out to see her standing at the end of the alley.

"I BET YOU WON'T EVER MESS OVER ANOTHER WOMAN AGAIN!" she yelled

"Crazy Bitch!"

Nathaniel shakes his head, and lowers the garage door.

He reaches his master bedroom and immediately strips down for a shower. Water has always soothed his nerves ever since he was a child. He loved swimming when he was younger and he was good at it too, until Rachel forbade him to go, for whatever reason she had; he never asked. He jumps out the shower and wraps a towel around himself. Not caring that he's still wet, he lies across his California king bed and turns his sixty inch television to ESPN.

"Fuck this I need a drink." He says climbing out of bed. Walking to the mini bar in his bedroom, he stumbles over his clothes on the floor. "Now this is about the only time I need a wife; to clean up my mess." He snatches his vest up causing Dr. Washington's card to fall at his feet. He picks it up and rolls his eyes. "After what just happened, maybe I should give you a call after all." He retrieves his cell phone and crawls back into bed. "Well here goes nothing." He hesitantly dials the number.

"The strong do what they have to do and the weak accept what they have to accept."

~Thucydides

~Gail~

"Gail, are you sure you don't want me to go with you to see Dr. Erickson? Zaya ask as she watches her friend struggle to put on her heels.

"Yes Zaya I'm sure, I told you I'm a big girl, I'll be fine. Besides, don't you have a lunch date with that lawyer guy you met the other day?"

Zaya looks at Gail and rolls her eyes.

"Girl he cancelled about an hour ago."

"What? This is the third guy to either cancel or stand you up this month."

Shaking her head, Gail continues.

"Baby girl, we're going to find you a real man."

"Look none of that is important right now. I'm more concerned with your well-being, than with a stupid guy," said Zaya.

She gets up from the receptionist desk to assist Gail with her shoes.

"See look at you... can't even put your shoes on. You're not fooling anyone; you are a nervous wreck!"

Gail tries to hide the tears but she didn't turn away in time. In a split second, tears were resting in the palms of her hands.

"Gail, look at me; I'm here for you. Whatever the results may be, I'm here. Everything will work out for the best" said Zaya.

"Thank you Zaya, I don't know what I'd do without you. It's just been so hard. You know with the divorce, running my practice, plus not knowing if I'm going to live or die from cancer. I've been a total mess!" explained Gail.

Zaya snatches her purse from behind her desk and walks over to the office door.

"Zaya..."

"Gail I don't want to hear another word. This is not up for discussion. I'm going with you and that's it!"

Gail throws up her hands and follows her stubborn friend outside.

The wait wasn't nearly as long as it was to receive the last results, so when Dr. Erickson walked into his office 10 minutes after their arrival, Gail knew it had to be good news, but the sadness in his eyes told her otherwise.

"Hi Ollie, so what do we have here & what's our next step?" inquires Gail.

"Gail the cervical cancer has reached late stage; which is stage IV or stage IVB. The malignancy has moved into other areas of the body. Like the abdomen, and intestinal tract. When the cancer has reached this stage, a radical hysterectomy may be performed as therapy. During this procedure, the uterus and much of the neighboring tissue, including the upper section of the vagina and internal lymph nodes are removed. In extreme cases, all of the organs in the pelvis, including the rectum and the bladder are also removed. Commonly, radiation treatments are used when cervical cancer has spread beyond the pelvis..." explained Dr. Erickson.

He stops speaking when he sees the tears streaming down both Gail and Zaya faces. Clearing his throat he continues.

"Gail that's not all, chemotherapy drugs may also be used to help fight late stage cervical cancer. The drugs could be pills or medicine given through an IV tube. Whatever we choose to do, it has to happen now."

Zaya broke the awkward silence.

"Dr. Erickson, what is the survival rate or life expectancy with treatment and without it?" asked Zaya.

"Because of the level of advancement, the survival rate is seventeen percent. Which gives you about six months to a year to live, Gail I'm sorry..."

That is the last thing Gail hears before everything fades to black.

Gail is awakened by someone softly saying her name.

"Gail, Gail honey, can you hear me?"

She opens her eyes to see her mother hovering over her.

"Mom, what are you doing here? What happened?"

"Zaya called me and your father and told us to get to Dr. Erickson's clinic immediately, because you had fainted" replied Gail's mother.

"Yeah sweetie, they just told us to get here, but wouldn't tell us why you fainted. They told us that you should tell us" said her father.

Gail looked around Dr. Erickson's office to see two pairs of gloomy eyes, another two pair with concern in them, and the other pair of eyes were glued to the floor; their owner was too ashamed to look at her. Slowly lifting herself onto her elbows, she glares at her father.

"Dad, I think you should sit down" suggested Gail.

Dragging herself off of the couch, she stations herself in the middle of the room so that she could address her parents and her backstabbing brother Monroe all at once.

"About three weeks ago I received a phone call from Dr. Erickson's nurse Veronica,

to come into the clinic to receive the results
from the colposcopy that I previously had
done. To make a long story short, Dr. Erickson
informed me that I have cervical cancer and
that we needed to see what stage it was in.
Well we did more testing and come to find out;
I'm in the final stage of this cancer."

Holding back tears, Gail continues.

"The survival rate for me is seventeen
percent; which gives me six months to a year
to live."

"Oh Lord my baby!"

Gail's father catches his wife as she collapses.
Monroe suddenly looks ill as he holds his
stomach and slowly lowers into a chair.
Helping his wife onto the office couch, Gail's
father approaches Dr. Erickson.

"Please Dr. Erickson; is there anything
that can be done for my baby girl?"

"Mr. Shannon, if she chooses we can do
a radical hysterectomy; we could put her on
chemotherapy drugs as well," replied Dr.
Erickson.

"Ollie, would I still be able to run my
practice and live a decent life, or will this
procedure and drugs make me too weak to
function normally?" asked Gail.

"Well it depends on the type of chemotherapy drug we choose. Some will make you vomit or feel nauseated. You may experience hair loss and diarrhea, along with dizziness, headaches and drowsiness, just to name a few of the many side effects. The good thing is, not all of them are long term, some of them are fairly short." he responds.

Making up her mind right then and there that she didn't want to spend her last days' sick and miserable, she turns to look at her parents.

"I'm sorry mom and dad, but I don't want to pop pills or have an IV in my arm every other day for the rest of my short life. I want to live and be happy for once. I want to be free of all responsibilities and just have fun. I've worked hard and played none my entire life and I'll be damned if I leave here never knowing what it's like to be genuinely happy."

She walks over to her doctor and gives him a huge hug.

"Thank you Ollie for everything, but I will not be seeking treatment."

Monroe jumps out of his seat.

"GAIL YOU HAVE GOT TO BE KIDDING ME? YOU CAN'T BE SERIOUS RIGHT NOW.

THIS IS YOUR LIFE WE ARE TALKING ABOUT HERE," he yells.

"Please Gail... don't do this," pleads Dr. Erickson.

Zaya had heard and seen enough.

"I can't believe you, how could you be so selfish? You have people in this room who love you and many others out there that love you and you're just giving up on life like this? What happened to practice what you preach? Every day you tell distraught individuals that there's always a chance for a better tomorrow and that nothing is impossible with God on your side. If you're not helping someone communicate better with their loved ones, then you're helping them to learn how to love and appreciate themselves. You do these things for complete strangers but you're refusing to do the same for yourself. Well Gail Latrice Washington, I will not sit back and watch you slowly deteriorate, when you get some damn sense call me, until then... we're done; we will do business that's it, that's all."

Zaya mumbles something along the lines of 'this is pure foolery' as she exits Dr. Erickson's office. Ollie sees the perfect opportunity to escape this drama and he takes it.

"Obviously you guys have a lot to discuss. You can use my office for as long as you like. I'll be up front seeing other patients."

Gail waits for Dr. Erickson to leave before explaining her decision to her family.

"I'm sorry everybody, I know this decision is a rash decision and it doesn't make much sense to you. But if you know me, which all of you do, then you know every decision I make is final. I've always been a very sure person, and this time is no different. Now you can walk out of my life like Zaya just did or you can help make my final time on this earth the best time I've ever had... it's up to you."

Gail's father embraces her before nodding his head signaling that he was going to be there for his only daughter.

"Baby I love you and you deserve to be happy, but I can't stand by and watch my little girl die. Please, will you please reconsider? For me, your mother, will you do that?"

Gail shakes her head no. Devastated by her daughter's decision, Mrs. Shannon runs crying out of the office, with Mr. Shannon not too far behind.

"Gail I think you should think about what you're doing."

"I'm trying to figure out why you even care. Hell, I want to know why are you even here. I mean, aren't you some married man's mistress around the clock? Please spare me the loving brother act, because loving you are not."

"Look Gail..."

"Boy please, go do what you do best and find somebody else man to fornicate with. The night is still young; you have plenty of time and victims to choose from."

She leaves Monroe behind, mouth wide open from the shock of her words.

> *"The whole world can become the enemy when you lose what you love."* ~*Kristina McMorris*

~Raven~

Even though Zaya isn't talking to Gail, she still maintains a professional attitude at work. It's tearing her apart that she's not speaking to her good friend, but what Gail is doing is hurtful and selfish. Or is she the one being hurtful and selfish? Her friend is running out of time and she's walking around with an attitude because she doesn't want her to go without a fight. Maybe that's what's bothering her most about this whole thing; Gail isn't fighting for her life and she can't understand why. Well today she's going to find out the reason behind this unfathomable decision. Besides, it's been a couple of weeks since she's spoken to her friend and she is really beginning to miss her.

With her mother and close friend being upset with her, Gail has thought long and hard about her decision to just live and make the best out of the time she has left. She has spent countless sleepless nights trying to figure out what is her purpose in life. All she knows is that she has to do a good deed or two before she leaves this earth. Jilted out of deep thought by the sound of Zaya's voice, Gail gathered her notebook and sat in her favorite chair awaiting her first client of the day. Raven Robinson is the two time reigning champion of all four tennis majors. He's not only the top tennis player in the world; he's also her hardest patient to date. He was given an ultimatum by the International Tennis Federation after hitting an umpires chair with his racket; to either get help for his anger management or be banned from tennis forever. Raven's tough as nails with a wall of steel around his heart. She's been trying to break him down for three months now and still no progress. She's knows that there's a reason why not only tennis, but manipulation seems to be a game that he loves to play.

Gail takes a deep breath when the doorknob turns.

"Geeeeeeeeee Geeeeeeeeeeeeeee"

Gosh I hate it when he calls me that.

"Raven, how are you?" asked Gail.

"I'm good Gee Gee, just trying to stay sexy for the ladies. What have you been up to? You find another exercise to try to get to the root of me as you like to say?" asked Raven.

"Nope, no exercises today, I just want to talk; nothing more, nothing less" Gail responded.

"Gee Gee come on now, you know how I feel about this. Just ask me some questions so I can bounce."

"Okay Raven; who is the new lady in your life this week?" asked Gail.

"Kellie, Rebecca, Selena, Jasmine, Leslie, Gabrielle and Courtney."

"Hmm, why so many?"

"I like different flavors... plus I'm young, rich and famous. I can have whomever I want, whenever I want... however I want next question," he retorted.

"The last time you were here, you told me that you can, and I quote; make any woman do something strange for some change and then kick her to the curb. What I want to know is why do you have to use money to get some ass? You are a good looking man. Six four, dark, with bedroom eyes; the body of a God, intelligent and hilarious; I know women who would want you off of your looks alone."

Taken aback by his therapist rude question, Raven takes a few deep breaths before answering. Gail notices and quickly realizes that angering him is the key to getting to know the real him.

"I can get sex from any woman, any time of day just with this handsome face. You know Gee Gee, I kind of feel like you just took a shot at me, am I wrong?" he asked.

"Yes you are, I just asked a simple question. "

"Well I didn't like that one so ask a different one" said Raven.

Damn, I thought insulting him would make him angry enough to say what's on his mind.

"What was her name and how long ago was it when she broke your heart?"

That question made him choke on his bottled water.

Bingo.

"What makes you think my heart has been broken?" he questioned.

"Because of your behavior towards women, you treat them like they are a piece of meat. You have no respect for them at all; which is baffling to me because you love your mother and grandmother to death. So either you lied about having a good relationship with the women in your family, when in all actuality deep down inside hate the female species or you were deeply wounded by someone you were deeply in love with. Which one is it?" inquired Gail.

Gail watches as her last question causes his jaw to tighten and a vein to appear in his forehead.

"Well it's been real, gotta go."

"Wait a minute Raven. Can you just answer that one question for me, who is she?"

He releases the doorknob and sits back down onto the couch.

"Her name is Trinity... Trinity Trent."

"Hold on, isn't that Dale Trent's wife?"

"Yes, we were engaged three years ago, she left me for him. He had more money, and he was the number one male tennis player at the time, I was just up and coming. I didn't have the fame or the fortune. I spent every last dime I had on that damn engagement ring and she pawned it and bought some damn Jimmy Choo's and a handbag ain't that about a bitch? Well after that, I vowed to never give my all to another woman as long as I'm breathing. So you're right; they are nothing but purchased pieces of meat."

"That's why whenever you play against Dale Trent you demolish him, it's personal for you?" asked Gail.

"Yep, well I'm all done with all of this emotional spillage crap. See you next time Gee Gee."

Gail watches Raven scurry out of her office without looking back. She can tell that she hit a nerve and she plans on hitting it a lot more.

When he turns the corner, his two body guards Lance and Don were waiting for him by the front entrance.

Lance the tallest one of the duo, stood six foot six, dark as Wesley Snipes and buff like Dwayne Johnson, A.K.A the Rock. Don on the other hand looked like the R&B singer Ginuwine just six foot three with muscles that look like he lives at the gym.

"You ready boss?" asked Lance as he handed Raven his sunglasses.

"Yea, let's get out of here."

Raven climbed in the back of his hummer frustrated from the session he just had with Dr. Washington. He didn't like people prying into his business but that's the job of a therapist right, to be nosy.

"Where to boss?" asked Don

"Home, I want to rest before I take this long flight to London for the Wimbledon Championships."

The drive to his ten bedroom, five bath home in river forest, took all of forty-five minutes.

He is greeted by a thick, light skin, red head when he enters his home.

"Raven baby, dinner is ready." She said with a smile.

"Thanks Courtney, I have a question for you though, why do you have on so many clothes?"

"Oh I'm sorry baby, I'll fix that right now."

She began taking off her clothes, stripping right down to a pair of red thongs with black lace and a matching bra. She smiled when she seen how pleased he was with her.

"That's better. Go wait for me in the guest bedroom. I'll be up in a second."

"Yes baby," responds Courtney.

He drools as her ass jiggles as she walks up the stairs, occasionally looking back and licking her lips, letting him know that she was ready.

The scent of catfish, collard greens, baked macaroni & cheese, cornbread, sweet potatoes, and fried chicken invaded his nose. He knew it was only one person that could cook like that.

"Jasmine is my plate ready?!" he yelled into the kitchen.

"It sure is baby," she responds.

Jasmine is five foot five with the body of a goddess. She has big thighs with an apple bottom, a small waist and wore a double D cup. Her thick wavy hair stops just above her waist. She has almond shaped eyes with a hint of hazel in them, and a cute little cleft in her chin.

She serves him with two plates, one held soul food and the other held his favorite dessert, apple cobbler.

"Thank you baby, now why don't you come upstairs and feed this too me!"

With sex in her eyes, she leads him up to the bedroom, dropping a piece of her clothing along the way.

The next day he arrives in Wimbledon refreshed and confident. After all, he is the defending champion and he plans on raising that silver gilt cup and receiving that one point six million dollar check again.

He settles into his hotel suite and then heads to the practice courts with his coach, the renowned four time Wimbledon champion, two time US Open and French Open champion, and one time Australian Open champion; Paul Sails. His first round opponent is a young Frenchman by the name of Audric Debree. The kid is a scrappy young fella, but his shots have no power behind them, especially his two-handed backhand.

This match is going to be a piece of cake.

"Raven let's go, let's start off with a hitting session; forehands first." Instructed coach Sails.

He's known for his crushing forehands and speed so he was demolishing every ball his coach sent over the net.

"Don't look now Raven, but your favorite person just walked onto the court."

He knew who his coach was referring to but he couldn't help but turn around to see. There he was, Dale Trent, his arch nemesis. He hated his guts and proved it time and time again by smashing him in the finals of all four majors. He'd beaten Dale like he stole something, in all actuality he did. He plans on history repeating itself again. Raven just shook his head.

I know this dude not walking over here trying to interrupt my practice session. Yep, he is.

"What's up Robinson, I just came to tell you that Trinity says 'Hello."

"Tell her I don't speak to sluts."

"Hold on, did you just call my wife a slut?"

Dale steps into Raven's face, Raven positions himself even closer touching Dale's nose with his.

"I can say it in another language if you need me to, how about Swahili?"

"Do it and see what happens" Dale threatens.

"Boy I'll smack those words right back into your mouth, keep talking."

"Aye come on now boys, save it for the match." said coach.

Dale backs away mean mugging Raven. It takes everything in Raven to not knock the shit out of Dale, but he didn't want to get disqualified for fighting on the premises.

"Raven look at me, you know what you have to do right?" asked his coach.

"Yea I do. I'm a whip his ass like his mama should have. He thought it was personal before, he hasn't seen shit yet."

"We all have an old knot in the heart we wish to untie." ~*Michael Ondaatje*

~Zaya~

"Gail, Mr. Thompson has cancelled his appointment for the day, so you are free from twelve forty-five until one thirty." Zaya spoke into the intercom.

"That's perfect Zaya, I wanted to chat with you alone anyway."

The hell she wants to chat with me for?

"Okay, let me just straighten up my desk a little and I'll be in there."

Zaya stacked her files neatly and had all of the calls transferred to Gail's office before heading in there.

Knock! Knock!

"Come on in Zaya, have a seat."

"Hey Gail, what's up?"

"How are you doing friend? We haven't really sat down and talked since your outburst at doctor Erickson's office."

"Yea well, I was taken aback by your rash decision to not fight for your life. I mean, you don't find that a least bit selfish Gail? You may not love yourself or care about yourself, but I do, so do your parents and brother believe it or not. Monroe is devastated you're just letting your life slip away like this."

"Besides my demise Zaya, what else is bothering you?"

"What do you mean what else is bothering me? Nothing! Why can't I just be pissed off that my good friend is slowly committing suicide, rather she wants to admit it or not."

"How's your love life Zaya? Ever since you broke your engagement off with Kenneth, you've been striking out with men. Either they stand you up or drop off the face of the earth that has to be tough for you."

"Oh I'm sorry, I don't remember signing up for a session with Dr. Washington. Excuse me but I have work to do."

"Zaya wait, sit down. I assure you my intentions are not to upset or offend you. I just want to know why a smart beautiful woman like yourself, is having the worst luck with men? You are a college graduate, no children, never been married, a great cook, and have a big heart. Zaya you have the prettiest smile that I've ever seen. Your big brown eyes are inviting and your skin is damn near as perfect as mines. Hell if I was a lesbian I would definitely try to get with you."

Zaya plops down onto the couch laughing at her boss's colorful description of her.

"Gail I don't know; I wish I had an answer for you. It's just that, I meet a great guy and I think to myself; he could be the one, the one I deserve to have."

"Maybe that's the problem Zaya, you approach every relationship with high expectations and you shouldn't. Some people are only in your life for a season, nothing more, and nothing less. It's like your pressing for the next man to fill a void created by Kenneth. With that mentality, you're going end up disappointed every time."

"But dammit Gail I'm supposed to be married right now! How could he betray me this way? He ruined my fairytale."

Gail sits next to her friend on the couch and hands her a tissue.

"Zaya you have everything a man could ever want in a wife, you just have to be patient and stop walking around with an 'I want to get married' sign on your forehead, and you are scaring men away. You want them to run to you not from you. I think you should call Kenneth, you need some closure."

"Please, I almost barbequed the man, he doesn't want to talk to me."

"Trust me, it will help if you tell him how what he did made you feel. You need to put this to rest Zaya. If you don't, your luck with men isn't going to change. You need to let this go so you can work on bettering yourself."

Sighing, "I guess you're right."

Gail laughs, "I know I'm right. Now tell me everything that happened that night, you never really went into detail."

Zaya went on to tell Gail about that heart wrenching night and how she almost killed her fiancé.

"Yea girl, I seen him humping her and everything went black. His best friend Jake said that I grabbed some green rubbing alcohol off his dresser threw it on Kenneth and that slut and then tried to set them on fire with a lighter I retrieved from my purse. I never got the chance because Jake tackled me to the floor before I could spark the lighter."

Gail burst into laughter.

"Gail that's not funny! I could be in the big house right now for blazing those two idiots. A few months after that, I found out that she was pregnant with his child. I saw his mother in a grocery store and she told me."

Zaya can't help but to laugh along with Gail about that crazy experience.

"Okay okay, I'm sorry for laughing. I was just picturing you getting violent, and it's cracking me up. But in all seriousness Zaya, there is someone for everyone. Your husband is out here somewhere, just be patient, trust me."

Zaya studies Gail's face before speaking.

"Gail I just wish... I just wish you had the love in your life that you deserve. You're a good woman, a good person. I can't understand why Chaz and Monroe would hurt you the way that they have. It amazes me how you continue to show love for others with all that's going on in your world. Damn Gail, I love you. I don't want you to die."

Gail hugs Zaya and they begin to cry, while telling each other how much they love one another.

"I love you Zaya. You're on the top of my list of good deeds, you better believe that."

"When you are guilty it is not your sins you hate, but yourself."~ Anthony De Mello

~Gail~

"Okay enough of the mushy stuff Zaya, let's get back to work!" Gail smiled to herself when she thought of how much her good friend loved her. Zaya is one of the most honest, realest people she's ever met and it sure warmed her heart to know that she was loved.

"Gail, Chaz is here, do you want to see him?"

Chaz, what the hell is he doing here?

"Um, yea Zaya send him back." replied Gail.

When Chaz walked through the door, she is in complete shock. The once well-groomed man she loved looks like a derelict, he looks rough and dirty. She can't help but to think that whatever he's going through; he deserves it. All of the women calling her home at all times of night, the STD's, all of the lonely nights because he was supposedly working late.

The sight of him makes me sick, too bad I don't have my .22.

"Hi Gail, how are you?"

"What can I do for you Chaz? We're not supposed to meet up until next week, with our lawyers present."."

"Yea I know I just wanted to see you. Well I more so needed to see you Gail, may I sit down?"

She motioned for him to have a seat.

"Chaz if you came here to convince not to go through with the divorce, you're wasting your time. I have every intention to..."

"I know Gail, but just hear me out." Before he could continue he began to cough uncontrollably, he grabbed a tissue from a Kleenex box sitting on the coffee table.

"Chaz are you okay? You look horrible." Asked Gail.

"Yea I'm okay, I just have this flu that won't go away. I've had it maybe a week after our incident."

"You sure it's the flu Chaz? I don't think the flu last for more than two weeks and it's been well over that."

"I have an appointment in a few days, I'll have some test ran. Gail I spoke with Monroe and he told me what you're doing and I came here to make a proposal."

"Do you keep in touch with all of the people you've cheated on me with?"

"I didn't come here for that; I came here to make a deal with you."

"A deal, what kind of deal are we talking about Chaz?" inquired Gail.

"Well, I've thought long and hard about this and I think what I'm asking of you is pretty reasonable." He wiped his nose and continued.

"I will only sign the divorce papers under one condition; and that is allow me to be here for you during your final days Gail right up to the end."

Is this fool on drugs?

"Is this a joke, because I am not amused?"

"This is not a joke. Gail I love you, always have. I know I wasn't the best boyfriend or the best fiancé and I damn sure wasn't the best husband; but through it all, you never left. God Gail, I gave you so many reasons to walk out on me and you stayed, I've never been loved so much by anyone my entire life. I guess what I'm saying is; I didn't love you the way that you deserved to be loved because I don't know how. I don't know how to show a person that I love them. I feel so bad that I let my tainted upbringing ruin you, ruin us. I feel solely responsible for what you're going through. I gave you HPV; and that sexually transmitted disease can cause cervical cancer. Please Gail, I feel like I owe you, let me be here for you."

Gail looks at him completely taken aback and angered by his request.

"So basically, you want me to help you get over the guilt you feel for making my life a living hell. This is clearly not about being here for me in my time of need, it's more so about you soothing your own mind. Your conscious is eating you alive and you can't take it anymore. Once again Chaz, you're using me for your own selfish reasons. Get the hell out of my office."

"You know, that's exactly what my uncle use to say to me after he was done sodomizing me; get the hell out of my office."

What the hell?

"Say what? You were molested as a child? How come you never told me?"

"Who goes around telling people that their uncle made them come into his home office to fulfill his sick fantasies? He took pictures and gave me ten dollars like I was a cheap thrill. There were days I couldn't even sit down..." Chaz covered his face with his hands and rocked back and forth.

Gail walks over to him, reluctantly placing her hands on his shoulders.

"Finish Chaz, what were you going to say?"

He lifts his head and looks into her eyes before speaking.

"You had to know. You had to know that something was off with me."

"I didn't think this. I mean there are a lot of straight men that get manicures and pedicures. There are a lot of straight men that wear fitted clothing and love romance movies. You sure in the hell didn't lack in the bedroom, you did things to my body that no man has ever done. It wasn't like you were flamboyant with it, how in the hell was I supposed to know? Sure you're sensitive but that's what I liked most about you. Now what were you going to say?"

"He used to call me a faggot when he's the one that turned me into one, he said that I enjoyed it because I would climax when we would... you know."

"How old were you when all of this started?"

"I was thirteen and he was like forty when we started having sexual intercourse, but I was eight when the inappropriate touching began. God this is hard for me, can I have a glass of water?"?" asked Chaz.

Gail retrieves a pitcher of water and a cup from her desk and pours him a cup.

"Did you ever tell your parents? If so, what was their reaction?"

"I told them and my dad smacked the crap out of me and called me a liar. My mother believed me, she just didn't say so."

"Well how do you know that she believed you?"

"She turned pale when I told her, like it has happened to her as well."

"Your uncle, is he your mother's brother?"

"Yes, he's her oldest brother. Many years later on her death bed she told me that he broke her virginity when she was fourteen and he was nineteen. The day before she died, we shared our deepest and darkest secrets with one another. She cried and apologized repeatedly after I told her what happened on my sixteenth birthday, but I don't want to open that door again."

"Chaz you've come this far; you might as well get it all out. Please tell me, what happened on your sixteenth birthday?"

"My uncle and his friend forced me to partake in a threesome. He would always threaten that he'd send pictures to all of my father's friends and my school mates if I ever told or refused him., So when he told me to meet him in the basement to get my birthday present, I did what I was told. Everyone one was upstairs eating, laughing and having a good time at the party my mom threw for me, so I slipped down into the basement undetected. When I reached the bottom of the stairs his friend Larry was sitting in a chair stroking his penis. I was instructed to take my clothes off and give head to Larry. When I started to, my uncle came up behind me and penetrated me. They took turns until they were both satisfied. They both tossed twenty dollars at me and said happy birthday and went back upstairs. I was never the same, I felt unloved and cheap. I felt dirty and disgusting, I felt alone Gail. So I lashed out sexually; I've cheated on every person I've ever been with. I thought if I dated women that I could erase these urges I have to be with a man. When I met you I just knew that you were the one, but I was fooling myself I used you to appear heterosexual and I'm sorry."

Gail walks over to her office window overwhelmed by what she was hearing.

"Gail I'm so sorry for what I've put you through. You didn't deserve any of it. Please let me make it up to you. I swear this is not all about me, I owe you. I owe you so damn much."

"If you're so sorry then why are you still in contact with my brother?"

"He didn't tell you? He would leave me to do all of the dirty work."

"Tell me what?"

"Monroe and I are in a relationship. We've been together ever since you kicked me out, but Gail that doesn't change how I feel about you, please think about my offer."

"So you're telling me that you want me to forgive you and become best of friends with you while you're still sleeping with my baby brother?"

"Well when you say it like that, it makes me seem like a selfish bastard" replied Chaz.

He joined her and glared out the window.

"Gail, please find it in your heart to forgive me, you are right, this guilt is eating me alive. You've always been there for me, let me return the favor."

She turns away and buzzes her secretary.

"Zaya, can you see Mr. Washington out please?"

"Gail, please..."

"Chaz I have to think about this, this is too much. I'll give you a call, email you or something but right now, you need to go."

"Okay, I understand. I hope to hear from you Gail."

Gail watches the tears fall down her soon to be ex-husbands face as he exits her office. Zaya mouth the words, 'Are you okay' and she shakes her head yes before shedding a few tears of her own.

"Grief does not change you, it reveals you."~ John Green

~Morgan~

Morgan pulls up to her hair salon in a brand new Fuchsia Continental GT speed Convertible blasting Beyoncé's 'Bow down'; turning the heads of haters and admirers posted up at neighboring businesses. She can care less about what people think or say about her, she's worked hard for everything she has, well pretending to love men with money was a job in itself. The luxury car, the big house and her thriving business all came from her popping, locking, and dropping it. She walks up to the entrance and looks it over; yep, 'In Hair Salon and Spa' was her baby. No amount of rumors, gossip and other high school drama is going to deter her from being whom she is... and that's a boss.

The salon is overflowing with customers; women getting sew-ins, pin-ups & cuts, having glasses of wine while being serviced or waiting to be seen by their beautician.

"Good morning Nikki, who do I have and what would they like done today?"

"Good morning Ms. Cloud, three out of your four appointments cancelled today. Toya went into labor, Alicia is hung over from club hopping last night and Wendy's car broke down so she had to use her hair money to get it fixed, she was pissed."

"I know she was, you know Wendy don't play about two things: her appearance and her finances. I'm going to give Toya's husband a call to see how she's doing and Alicia stays hung over, I'm not fooling with her wild tail. Okay so who's here now?" Morgan asked her receptionist.

"Your favorite client in the whole wide world!"

"Who? Stop playing with me Nikki. I know you're not talking about who I think you're talking about?"

"Yep Glory is here and she's sitting right there in your chair waiting for you."

Morgan takes a deep breath and shakes her head.

"Didn't I tell this broad not to ever step foot in this salon ever again? Why in the hell is she here?"

"I don't know Ms. Cloud, why don't you go over there and find out. Now Morgan, count to twenty and sing kum ba ya, you said you were done slapping whores."

Morgan rolls her eyes and slowly walks back to her station.

"Good luck with that!" yelled Nikki.

As she approaches her station, Morgan catches Glory going through drawers and cabinets.

"Um excuse me, but why are you going through my things Glory? Matter of fact, why are you even here?"

"Because Morgan, I left a few hair clips the last time I was here and I want them back."

"The lost and found box is up front at the receptionist desk, so whatever you're looking for go look for it up there. Thank you and good bye." said Morgan

"Wait, I'm sitting in your chair for a reason, so I'm going to need you to be professional for once in your life, Now I want a..."

Everyone in the salon turns and looks at Morgan. Embarrassed and fed up, she steps out of her stilettos and spin Glory chair around so she could face her.

"Now you want a what, a busted lip? Now I'm going to tell you one more god damn time to get your trifling, rumor spreading, hating, slutty ass up out of my shop or else I'ma drag you up out of here by that synthetic weave of yours, do you understand me Glory?"

"Come on Morgan, why can't the past be the past? Yes I was a regular at your shop even though I was banging your fiancé the entire time you two where together. And yes I banged him the day that he died. Don't you think I feel bad too? He died in my bed. It was extremely painful for me to tell you what happened, that's exactly why I waited until you finished my press and curl because I didn't want you to burn my shit off. It took me years to get my length back and I just couldn't risk it."

No she didn't!

Morgan hit Glory with a right uppercut and a left hook before dragging her through the salon to the front door. All of the ladies jumped out of their chairs and followed Morgan with their cell phones recording the drama.

"OH MY GOD MORGAN, LET HER GO!" Nikki yelled as she tried to loosen Morgan's grip on Glory's hair.

"Let me go Nikki! She has lost her damn mind! Coming into my business talking crazy to me, I'm giving her what she asked for!"

She slings a kicking and screaming Glory out the door and onto the pavement. Morgan sits on top of her and starts punching and elbowing her until one of the men from the barber shop next door pulls her off.

"Morgan what the hell is going on? Let her go!"

"No Tim! Let me go! She comes in here bragging about sleeping with my deceased fiancé like I'm a lame or something. I had to give her what she asked for and I'm not done, so put me down!"

"Nope I'm not putting you down until you calm down." said Tim.

"Okay, okay I'm good you can let me go."

She broke free of Tim and walks over to Glory lying on the ground.

"You're lucky Tim pulled me off of you, because I was about to put you to sleep. Come back into my shop again if you want to and I promise on the Father, the Son and the Holy Spirit you will leave out on a stretcher.

Somebody get this trash from in front of my place of business."

She retrieved her handbag from her station and called her therapist.

"The Healing Center, this is Zaya speaking."

"Hey Zaya, this is Morgan, tell Gail I need to see her like right now, girl I almost committed a murder."

"What? Girl hold on let me tell her!"

Everyone was starting to pile back into the salon ranting and raving about what just went down.

"Dang Morgan you beat the bejesus out of her. I bet she won't come back in here acting crazy anymore!" said one of the customers.

"Shoot, I know not to play with Morgan, she might smack the black off me" said another customer.

"Shush! Be quiet y'all I'm on the phone. Yea Zaya, Gail can see me? Good I'm on my way."

Morgan made it to the Healing Center in record time. It usually takes her thirty minutes to get there but she arrived in half that.

"Hey Zaya, is she ready for me?"

"Yes, go right in."

She entered Gail's office only to be welcomed in by a stranger. She knows that it's Gail but she looks exhausted and frail, she looks terribly ill.

"Come on in Morgan, have a seat and stop staring at me like I'm a ghost."

"I'm sorry, you just look different, is everything alright? You look worn down."

"I'm fine, nothing I can't handle. How are you? Zaya said you almost went to jail, what's going on?"

"Gail I lost my mind, I beat the crap out of Glory and I wouldn't have stopped hitting her if my friend Tim, who has a barber shop next door to mines didn't pull me off her. I could've really hurt her Gail, like really, really hurt her."

"Glory, the woman that was sleeping with your fiancé Quentin?"

"Yes that trick. She came into my shop and wanted me to do her hair, talking about the past is the past, so what she slept with my fiancé and so what he died in her bed."

"Oooo no she didn't! And that's when you lost your temper?" asked Gail.

"No I asked her nicely to leave but she went on to tell me that she would've told me that he had died sooner but she didn't want me to burn the back of her neck with the hot comb; and that's when I lost my temper."

"Wait a minute! She said that? Lord have mercy! What happened next?"

"I started beating that ass that's what happened next! I wrapped my hand in her ten-dollar weave and drug her behind up out of there."

"So how do you feel about all of that? How do you feel about what she said to you and your reactions to it?"

"I feel angry, hurt, betrayed, sad, and ashamed. I shouldn't have let her take me there but damn Gail, the things she said hurt so bad, I just couldn't take it."

"Have you ever visited Quentin at his grave site and told him how his death and the whole thing with Glory makes you feel? Or have you looked at a photo of him and began expressing your emotions to him? I think it's about time that you vent and tell him how his infidelities and passing has caused you great pain. He wasn't perfect Morgan, hell none of us are, but just because we aren't perfect doesn't give us a pass for ruining people. Just because he's no longer living does not mean you have to pretend that he was an angel." stated Gail.

"I know, but I was always taught not to speak ill of the dead. I don't want to remember all of the bad he's done to me. I want to remember the vacations, the passionate love we made, and the cute names we chose for our future children. I prefer not to think about all of the girls that called my phone at all times of the night or sent me threatening emails. I don't want to remember all of the fights and arguments Gail."

"So do you like the person you have become since his passing? Because you were my beautician before you were my client and I remember a completely different Morgan. The Morgan I remember wasn't so hot tempered and didn't drain men's bank accounts like she does now."

"Look, these men aren't on my level, so I get whatever I can out of them before I toss them in the trash." replied Morgan

"Is it because they aren't Quentin? They aren't smacking you around, spending all of your money; they aren't degrading you, making you feel worthless, because that's what I remember the most about your relationship with him. Why aren't they on your level Morgan?

"Quentin had his flaws, but his pros outweighed his cons. I believed he was one of a kind."

"So his looks and sex was enough to deal with his cheating and constant disrespect? Let me tell you something Morgan, do you know why I stayed with my husband after his countless affairs outside of our marriage? I stayed with him because I was afraid to start over again. When you've given your all to someone for so long, it's hard to move on. When you've bared your soul, shared your fears and darkest secrets with someone that claimed to love you, it's makes you dismiss the possibility of ever opening up to someone like that ever again. Morgan I don't think the men aren't good enough, I think you are scared of starting over and everything that comes with it. You are being emotionally elusive and breaking hearts not because these men aren't on your level, it's because you're afraid to let anyone that close to you again. You've created a pattern that I've noticed."

"A pattern?" asked Morgan.

"Yes a pattern, you date a guy for 3 months and then you dump him for whatever goofy reason you can come up with at the time."

"Excuse me but I've had good logical reasons for letting those men go Gail, you don't think so?"

"Morgan you dumped Kristopher because his hands were too soft."

"Gail I'm a woman, I don't want no man that get more manicures than I do."

"Okay well what about Joseph, you dumped him because he wouldn't shave his chest hair. I don't care what you say, that was silly!"

"He always wanted me to lie on his chest, felt like I was smothering my face in a sweaty vagina, no thank you!"

Gail threw her pencil at Morgan as they laughed at the mental picture her last comment gave her.

"All I'm saying is I need you to get off of that high horse and go into dating without all of that extra baggage. If not, you'll be searching for a Quentin replacement for the remainder of your life. Morgan you deserve more. You deserve to be loved and treated with respect. I know you want to be in love again, don't you?"

"I sure do Gail, I'm just afraid like you said. Ugh! I hate when you're right! You make me sick! Let me get out of here before you want a hug and kiss and shit."

Morgan heads for the door as soon as Gail opens her arms and approaches her.

"Ugh! Get the hell on Gail, you know I don't do that mushy stuff."

"You are gorgeous and smart, you have the face of Jessica Alba and the business mind of Donald Trump and you know it. Gail opens the door for her, "All jokes aside Morgan, I really do care about you. I want nothing but the best for you."

"Aw damn, now I have to hug you for real!"

Morgan bear hugs Gail and gives her a kiss on the cheek.

"For these prices honey you better love me to death!" said Morgan.

She thanks Gail and says her goodbyes.

"You know what Gail is right. I should go visit Quentin and get all of this anger off my chest. I mean he can't talk back which could be viewed as a good thing. I wouldn't have to yell shut the hell up let me finish, because he's interrupting me like he would like to do. Yea Quentin, I think we need to have a little talk once and for all."

"Those who aim at great deeds must also suffer greatly."~ Plutarch

~Gail~

Gail arrives home exhausted from the day's events. Even though she's glad that she could talk some sense into Zaya and Morgan, Chaz's unexpected visit brought out emotions that she's worked hard to suppress. How dare he give her an ultimatum? Either she allows him to be a part of her life again or he's going to refuse to sign the divorce papers, what a chump. She was too tired and in too much discomfort to entertain his craziness, a shower and bed was the only thing on her mind. She rushed into the bathroom because she felt like she urinated on herself. She knew it was blood and not urine because she's been bleeding like she's on her menstrual for the past week.

"Dammit, this is the third pad I've used today. Lord please let this hot shower soothe my body; I don't know if I can take another night like the last few days." The pelvic and back pain, along with a swollen right leg has been keeping her up at night. She went grocery shopping two weeks ago and she's barely eaten any of it because she hasn't had much of an appetite. "Ollie said I would experience these symptoms. I guess you never believe certain things until they happen." She finally got the water to a comfortable temperature before stepping in. Immediately a sharp pain shot through her abdomen causing her to fall to the shower floor. "Ahhh, Oh My God!" She pulls herself up and drags herself to the bed; crawling under the covers holding her belly grimacing from the pain. "Maybe some extra strength Tylenol will knock out this pain." As she was getting out of bed she remembered that Tylenol was the one thing on her grocery list she forgot to get. "Damn! Forget it, time to get drunk." She went downstairs to the kitchen and raided her wine bar. She popped the cork on a nineteen ninety six Kistler Pinot Noir and took it straight to the head. "Pinot Noir, Chaz's favorite, okay Chaz you want to make threats and demands, well I have a few of my own." She got her laptop off the kitchen table and starts for the bedroom, abruptly stopping at the kitchen entrance. "I think I should take another bottle of wine for this."

For the past hour she's been staring at her Gmail new message box. After taking the final swig of wine from the second bottle she finally began typing.

Chaz,

I initially wanted to tell you to kiss my ass but I've changed my mind. Why, I don't know, but I have. Today you showed me a side of you that I've never seen before. You were vulnerable and open with me about how your childhood molded you into the man you are today, and in some weird way I feel like I should return the favor, and share my demons with you as you did with me. I lived with the devil and an angel, A.K.A Mom and Dad. Mom condemned me and dad praised me. I learned how to hate from her and I learned how to love from him. To her I wasn't pretty enough, smart enough, charming enough, hell I just wasn't 'enough' and she made sure to remind me every single day how much of a disappointment I was to her. But dad, well my daddy made me feel like I was more than just 'enough'. I worked hard in school so I could go to college early and I succeeded at that; I went to Loyola University to study Psychology on a full scholarship at the age of sixteen. I graduated with my Bachelors and Masters in five years; and soon after went on to achieve my PHD. You would think that would've satisfied my mother but it didn't, so I gave up on trying to please her. Even though my father showed me ample amount of love, I still had a void. That void caused me to look for love in all of the wrong places. Believe it or not I was a slut bucket in college. I slept my way around campus; students and faculty, I didn't care. I laid down and opened wide for anyone that showed interest in me; and when I say anyone I mean women. It took for me to get raped at a fraternity party to realize that being sexually generous wasn't going to make my mother show me the love that I pleaded and prayed for. The guy who violated me recorded the entire thing and shouted, "Listen to how she's moaning, I told y'all I could turn this dike straight; she loving this D" I was mortified. After that I remained celibate until I met you. Do you remember how we met? Well I do. I was walking down the Magnificent Mile with a bunch of folders in my hands, I was just leaving a meeting, when a gush of wind blew one of the folders out of my hands. I screamed obscenities and started chasing flying papers like a crazy fool. I looked to my right to see this tall, butterscotch colored man, with a fresh fade and the most beautiful big brown eyes that I've ever seen walking towards me with papers in his hands. You said, "I think that these belong to you." And I smiled and said, "Thank you so much sir." You said, "My name is Chaz Washington, not sir, what is your name?" I told you my name and then you proceeded to tell me how stunning I was and that you would love to take me out sometime. I never told you Chaz but I fell in love with you right then and there. When we dated it was great, but when you asked me to marry you I felt like the luckiest girl in the world. We were like white on rice with each other. We did everything together when you see one you surely would see the other. What happened to us? Why did our fairytale end? Everything we've ever done was with love and passion. I guess asking why and when did you fall out of love with me wouldn't make a difference now, but it is something I've been wondering for a while now. I've tried to pretend like we had it altogether, but I guess it was time for the charade to end. Through it all Chaz I never stopped loving you. People said I was crazy and weak for not divorcing you years ago, but dammit those vows meant something to me. I could've left after the STD, I could've left after all of the phone calls and emails I received from other women, but I wanted us to work. It's extremely embarrassing for a Psychologist not to be able to fix her own problems. To tell you the truth, I probably would've forgiven you again if this time wasn't with my little brother. Chaz how could you? My brother... well that was the straw that broke the camel's back, I was all done after hearing you moan his name. Yes, I snapped, but what was I supposed to do, join you? Sorry but I've had enough of you disrespecting me and our marriage and I had to let you know that, one way or another. I was finally getting use to the fact that I was going to die divorced and childless. God how I wanted to have children but it wasn't in God's plan for me to bare children and I've accepted that. I'm actually glad now that I wasn't able to get pregnant because I wouldn't want my babies growing up without a mother. Damn Chaz, why did you do this?! I loved you! Hell, I loved all of you. Anyways, Surprise, Surprise I forgive you Chaz, but I'm not sure if I can handle being in your presence especially since you're still freaking on my brother. So you have a choice; either you can sign the divorce papers and live happily ever after QUIETLY with Monroe or you can be known as the widow who's banging the brother of his deceased wife, it's up to you. I'm fine with whichever you choose.

P.S. ~ I'm serious as hell.

She closes her laptop and glances over at her phone and her alarm clock.

"It's twelve a.m. but I don't care, I'm about to call her, I have some things I need to get off my chest." She dialed her parent's home phone.

"Hello!" Answered the groggy voice on the other end.

"Mom we need to talk. Well I need to talk, you just need to listen."

"Gail what's wrong?"

"A lot mom, I'm dying and I'm getting a divorce, so I'm a little on edge. But those things aren't the reason I called. I called to tell you how unloved I felt by you growing up. You were so harsh, so hard on me, so damn mean to the point that I damn near had no kind of relationship. You made me feel less than a woman and I carried that disappointment with me throughout my life and it brought me nothing but heartache. You were a horrible mother, there's not one positive thing that you've done for me that you didn't benefit from. I went looking for love from strangers because of you. You know what? I can't do this, I have to go, good night mother."

"No Gail wait, you are right, I wasn't a good mother to you or your brother and for that I am so sorry. I didn't realize until the both of you were grown that I did to my children what my mother did to me. I thought gifts would make up for all of the wrong that I did and it has with Monroe but not with you. Baby I really wish you would reconsider on getting treatment, I really don't want to lose you Gail, and you are my baby."

"Mom I'm tired, I've been struggling and fighting my entire life. I've fought for your love and approval. I've fought to become a respected Psychologist in the city of Chicago. I've fought for my marriage. I've won one out of three, so excuse me if I'm all done with fighting. I just want to live and be merry. I want to do something great before I start transitioning mom."

"Like what honey?"

"I want to help the people that I love find true love. Zaya and Morgan are good friends of mine and they both deserve their Prince Charming or Night in Shining Armor. And Raven, he's hard on the outside and mushy on the inside. He refuses to admit to it but he wants to be a one woman man, not the playboy he portrays himself to be. I need to find a way to get them together, set up a way for them to meet and mingle with one another."

"Oh so you want to do what that Millionaire Matchmaker lady on television does, what's her name Patti or something like that? You know she throws these mixer thing-a-ma-jigs to get her clients to socialize with their potential husbands or wives?" said Mrs. Shannon.

It was like a light bulb lit up inside of her head, Gail knew exactly what she had to do.

"Hello Gail, are you still there?"

"Yea mom I'm here. I think I have an idea."

"Each of us has his own rhythm of suffering."~ Roland Barthes

~Nathaniel~

He's been standing outside the Healing Center for the past fifteen minutes trying to coach himself to go inside. *You're not crazy Nate, you're only doing this for your father, not because something is wrong with you, now go inside.*

"My name is Dr. Nathaniel Thompson and I'm here to see a Dr. Gail Washington."

Zaya looked up from her stack of papers to see a pair of hazel eyes staring at her.

"Yes Mr. Thompson, she'll be with you in a moment. Do I know you from somewhere?"

"Try again. That's a damn shame a grown woman can't come up with a better pick up line, yea I've used that one before."

Zaya did a double take.

"Say what? Pick up line? Chile please go have a seat somewhere."

"Yea pick up line, I seen the way you looked up at me, you think I'm gorgeous and well you're right. But I'm done dating women that can't match my bank account so sorry to crush your hopes and dreams, but I'm not interested."

This dude is over the top!

"Yea now I remember you. You're the dude that got into an argument with a chick across the street from here and she ended up smacking the hell out of you good for your ass."

"Another bitter woman, maybe it should be you going in there with the shrink and not me."

This fool has lost his got damn mind!

Zaya had heard enough, she called Gail heated.

"Gail if you don't get this I'm too sexy for myself muthasucka that's out here waiting for you, I'm a set it off up in here! Come get him, COME GET HIM!"

Zaya has never seen Gail move so fast in all of the years she's known her.

"Zaya what's wrong? Who do I need to get?" asked Gail.

Zaya points at Nathaniel.

"Mr. Thompson, please step into my office."

As Nathaniel trails behind Gail, he and Zaya have a stare down. Just before entering the office he whispers, "Bitter."

"I am not! But you're an asshole though!" Zaya yells.

"Mr. Thompson why don't you have a seat and tell me why my secretary was so worked up out there?"

"She's a bitter black woman like all of you are. Y'all blame men for your unhappiness when in all actuality if you all stayed in your place, you wouldn't have so many problems."

"And what's our place Nathaniel?"

"It's Dr. Thompson to you. See I'm a real doctor; you listen to people's problems for a living, that's not science, that's a talk show host."

Whew! Now I see why Zaya was pissed, I'm ready to kick him in the balls.

"Let me ask you something, do you talk to everyone like this? Do you purposely offend people like you're doing me?"

"Nope just women, all of you are worthless and useless. The only thing we really need you for is to birth our sons and give us a blow job on the regular."

"Is that what your mother did, give blow jobs on the regular to random men or did she give them to you?"

"Excuse me?"

"You heard me. Your mother, she did something to you, what was it and don't lie because your hate towards women is a clear sign that you have a mommy complex. So I'm going to ask again, what did she do to you?"

"Watch your mouth when you're talking to me, I'm a man, you need to show some respect Gail you..."

"And I'm a human being. If you want respect you have to give it, are you ever going to answer my question Nathaniel?"

"I'm only here because my father asked me to see you."

"Is that your final answer?"

"She use to abuse me when I was a child. There, are you happy now?"

"I'm sorry to hear that."

"Sure you are, you get paid to act like you care, when in reality you could care less." Nathaniel said.

"If you say so, how did she abuse you?"

"Damn you're nosy!"

"That's my job. Was it sexually or verbally?"

"Physically and verbally. She carved her initial into my lower back when I was a small boy all because I called her mama, she didn't like that."

He lifted up his shirt and showed Gail one of his bad memories. She approached him and ran her fingers across the keloid scar.

"This looks like an R, and she did this because you called her mama? What is her name?"

"Rachel... Rachel Porter."

"Wait a minute, is your father Nicholas Thompson? He's one of my clients."

"Yes, that's my dad. He gave me your card one day while we were having lunch. He said the same thing as you did, I treat women the way that I do because of Rachel. After finding a scorned woman waiting for me in my garage with a bat in her hand, I knew I had to make that call, so now I'm here."

"Nathaniel your father has told me so much about you, he's very proud of you. He's told me about every award, certificate and trophy that you've ever won in your lifetime. He is especially proud of the fact that you're one of the top pediatric surgeons in the United States. But what he's not proud of is how you demean women. He's deeply worried about you."

"Look I'm going to tell you like I told him, this is who I am, and I was made into this monster. You shouldn't be talking to me, you should be talking to Rachel."

"So you're telling me right here, right now that you've never not once wanted to be in love? You're telling me that you've never wanted to feel what it's like to have that special person to come home to after a long day of work? You've never wanted someone to cook you a hot meal, run you a warm shower and make love to you until you two pass out every single night? "

"Yea, yes I have. I just... you know what? I don't have to explain anything to you, I'm a grown man."

It was like a smack in the face.

Oh my God! He and Zaya are perfect for each other! She could love him and put him in his place at the same time! Why didn't I see this earlier?!

"This is true, you are a grown man and you're right, you don't have to explain anything to me but, the last time I checked, grown folks kept it real with themselves and you're not right now. I understand that we won't get to the root of everything in one session but I would like to ask you for a favor. I'm planning a party for singles, sort of like a mixer. It will be a chance to meet and socialize with a lot of other successful single people in the Chicago land. I would really love for you to stop through, I want you to think about it?"

"I'll think about it; you know, you're not so bad, I wish I could say the same for your girl out there."

Oh you will, just wait.

"Oh Zaya is cool, you'll see. Can I ask you for another favor?"

Nathaniel rolled his eyes.

"Nicholas told me about your mother and how she doesn't have long to go, would you consider going to see her? Maybe just tell her how you feel, just to have some kind of closure because you need it."

"I'll think about that too, good bye."

"Bye Dr. Nathaniel Thompson. I hope you really give what we've talked about some thought, take care of yourself, come back and see me if you ever need or want to."

Nathaniel nodded and closed the door behind him. He walked past Zaya's desk and shook his head.

Bitter.

"Stop shaking your head! I know what you're thinking and I'm not bitter!" said Zaya.

He drove around in circles before deciding to stop at the Lakeshore Rehabilitation Center where Rachel was. He sat there trying to calm his trembling hands by gripping the steering wheel tightly. "I'm a grown man, why am I afraid to see her?" He drifted off into a memory, one that he thought he packed away a long time ago. He was running around the living room with his paper airplane when he accidently bumped the end table and knocked over a glass giraffe, that glass giraffe just happened to be her favorite figurine. As soon as it crashed to the floor he knew that he was in for something terrible.

"You broke my giraffe? This was the only thing that my mother ever gave me and you broke it!"

"I'm... I'm sorry Rachel."

"You're sorry, boy sorry is not going to fix my giraffe. You know what, get your ass down there and count how many broken pieces there are."

He did as I was instructed and told her how many pieces there were. She then told me to take my clothes off and to get into the shower, so I did. Once I was wet, she came in with a belt and began to beat me.

"I'm going to hit your stupid ass for every piece of my giraffe that is on the floor!"

I screamed, begged and pleaded, but as usual, it made no difference. When she finally finished, I slowly sat down in the shower and cried while watching blood disappear into the drain with the water. The giraffe had shattered into twenty pieces.

"Forget this! Forget Rachel! Forget Gail! And forget Pops! I'm not doing this shit!"

He went to turn the key in the ignition when he felt something wet on his face. He looked into his rear view mirror to discover that he was crying. He took one last look at the Rehabilitation Center before pulling off.

"She can rot in hell."

"Shame is a soul eating emotion." ~
C.G. Jung

~Chaz~

"Chaz wake up, your phone is buzzing and it's getting on my nerves." Monroe says as he mounts him. He places Chaz's phone on his chest and begin to slowly kiss him from his chest to his crotch, taking all of him in his mouth.

"Mmmm only if you keep deep throating."

"No problem daddy."

Chaz unlocks his phone to find a notification email from Gail. He pushes Monroe off of him and swings his legs over the side of the bed, anxiously opening the message.

"No you didn't interrupt me to play on your damn phone Chaz. Whomever that is better have a better mouth piece than I do because no one pushes Monroe away. Chaz, do you hear me talking to you?"

"Oh my god Gail I had no idea..."

"Gail? What the hell is she doing contacting you, I know she doesn't want you back? She probably does knowing her weak ass."

Completely ignoring his lover's rude remarks, he reads on in disbelief at his ex-wife's confessions. He knew that she loved him but he had no idea how deep her love for him was. Monroe hugs him from behind and sticks his tongue inside of his ear trying to get his attention.

"Baby come on now, I'm horny, satisfy me please. I moved up here in the boondocks for a reason, I don't have to worry about the neighbors hearing me scream."

"I can't, I have to go."

"Excuse me, and where do you think you're going?" inquired Monroe.

"I need to talk to Gail if you don't mind?" replied Chaz.

"Actually I do mind, what the hell do you need to talk to her for? I know y'all are not talking about rekindling that dysfunctional ass marriage you two had."

"Monroe please miss me with the jealous and possessive act. We both know that you live in a crowded bed. All of us; me, Gail, and your parents have watched you whore yourself like you breathe air, you don't have a faithful bone in your body. Now if you excuse me, I need to go see my wife."

Infuriated, Monroe threw Chaz's shoes at him and everything else that he could get his hands on.

"You know what Chaz get the hell out of my house! You are just as pathetic as she is! You two were made for one another. I can't believe that you are leaving my bed to go and be up in a bitch face that can't satisfy you the way that I can and have. What does she have that I don't? Huh? What does she have that I don't Chaz?!"

Chaz looks over his shoulder with disgust.

"A heart, I shouldn't be here... I should've never been here Monroe."

"Chaz if you walk out of this house you better not ever come back! You will never find another person like me, trust and believe that!"

"I hope not, goodbye Monroe."

Chaz closed the bedroom door and muffled Monroe's obscenities. He rushed to his car and started in route to see Gail. With tears in his eyes, he held his cell phone in his hand trying to get up the nerve to call her. He had finally got up the nerve to dial her number but Monroe's call interrupted him.

"What Monroe? I'm not about to argue with you."

"Nobody walks out on me like that! Who do you think you are Chaz? I have pictures and recordings, if you don't get your ass back here I will post them to the internet and email them to every person you know, try me if you want to."

Chaz instantly became livid.

"Monroe play with me if you want to and I will break your little pretty ass in half, now YOU try me." He was so pissed that he didn't realize he was going over the speed limit.

"Kiss my ass Chaz!"

"No you kiss my.... SHIT!"

Chaz took his eyes off of the road for a split second, almost hitting a dog. He was inches from hitting the canine before he swerved left losing control of his car. He flipped four times before crashing into a tree. Monroe jumped at the sounds, he heard tires screeching and a big bang, but no Chaz.

"Chaz, Hello?! Chaz can you hear me?! Look Chaz I'm sorry! Would you please say something, I'm sorry."

"No man can think clearly when his fists are clenched."~ George Jean Nathan

~Raven~

Before every match he shuts himself off from the world; no phone, no television, no internet, just him and his thoughts. He hides inside his mind from outside distractions to remain focus on the task at hand and today was no exception. His alarm sounded off letting him know that it was time to head to Center Court.

"Welcome to the Wimbledon two thousand and thirteen championships semi-finals; I'm Katie Stash."

"And I'm David Steele. Today's match is an exciting one. We have Colin Murray from Great Britain whose ranked number three in the world up against the reigning champ and number one seed Raven Robinson. Katie, Raven hasn't lost one single match in the past two years, that's remarkable!"

"It sure is David, both men are quick on their feet and have devastating forehands. Colin's backhand is vicious and Raven's serve is impeccable, this should be a good one David."

"I agree Katie, both men make for some exciting tennis; the crowd is really in for a treat."

Raven and Colin meet at the center of the court for the coin toss with only the net separating them.

"Heads or Tails Raven?" asked the umpire.

"Heads serve, tails receive." The umpire says.

"Heads" says Raven.

He flips the coin and it lands on the grass court.

"Heads it is, Raven will have first serve."

Colin chose the side that they will play their first game on and they both begin to warm up for the match.

"And here we go ladies and gentlemen; the umpire has called time. The two thousand and thirteen Wimbledon semi-finals will start now." said commentator Katie.

"For the millions that are watching at home, you may not want to blink; you may miss something fantastic," said commentator David.

The match turned out to be every bit of what the crowd expected; both men grinding and dazzling their fans with a variety of shots and long exchanges. Even with Colin's aggressive playing style, Raven kept his poise and dominated his way to victory. The two men met up once again in the middle of the court, this time to shake hands after a grueling match.

"Damn man, I thought I had you for a second there."

Raven gave Colin a pat on the back, "They always do young blood... they always do."

They bowed to the crowd and signed a few autographs before going to do a press conference.

"Raven, Jeff here; it looked like Colin had your number in the final set, how did you manage to will yourself into a victory?" asked a journalist.

"I mentally smacked myself. I had to remind myself of who I am and what I am capable of; once I did that, it was a wrap." Raven says as he points to another journalist.

"Mark from Sports Life Magazine, Dale Trent came out on top today against the crafty Australian Blake Walker; can we count on another epic men's final from you two?"

"When have you ever known me to answer any questions concerning Dale? Today is no different. Thank you and see you all at the finals." replies Raven.

Raven exits the panel to find Trinity waiting for him outside of the conference room.

"Hey Rave, you looked good out there, how are you?"

"I'm good, do you need something?"

"No, well yes, I've wanted to talk to you for a while now, do you have a minute?" she asked.

"Not really, what do you want?"

"Rave I just want to apologize for how things went down with us. I was wrong, you didn't deserve what I did to you and I agonize over it every day. I truly regret walking away from us."

"Is this little confession here supposed to convince me to be easy on your punk ass husband when we play in the finals? If so you're wasting your time Trinity."

"No, no Raven listen, I came here to come clean to you. My conscious has been eating me alive, I have to clear the air once and for all."

"Come clean? Clear the air? What else did you do that you just need me to know?" inquired Raven.

"Yea baby, what else do you need him to know?" Dale walks up and joins the conversation.

"Hey Honey, I was just telling Raven that it was time that you two played nice for once. This war between you two has gone on for long enough." Trinity explains.

"Oh okay, I thought you were about to tell him about the baby," says Dale.

"Baby, what baby?" asks Raven.

"Your baby, the one I took her to kill" answers Dale.

Before Dale knew it Raven punches him square in the jaw. Everything went silent as Raven overwhelmed Dale with punch after punch, elbow after elbow. The journalist ran out of the conference room when they heard a woman screaming 'please stop'. It took four of them to pull Raven off top of an unconscious Dale.

"LET ME GO! I'MA KILL HIM! LET ME GO!" he finally snatches away and walks towards his ex.

"I gave you everything I had, I loved you, I wanted to marry you and you leave me for him. On top of that, you kill something that I've always wanted. You aborted my child without even talking to me first." He uses his index finger to lift up her head.

"Trinity, if I ever see you or him again, I promise you, you both will need an ambulance; I promise you that." Security rushes in and takes Raven away.

Raven knew he'd gotten himself kicked out of the tournament so he didn't even stick around to be told something that he already knew. When he lands back in Chicago with Don and Lance, waiting for him was, a gang of missed calls, text messages and voicemails; he only listened to one voicemail and that was Gail's.

Hey Raven it's me Gail, I just heard what happened on the radio. Call me if you want to talk, you know I'm always here. I'm not at the office so call me and I'll come to wherever you are okay? Bye."

"To the house boss?" ask Don.

"No, I want to drink and ride around the city all night, find a liquor store."

It was two a.m. in the morning and Gail's phone was ringing off the hook.

"Whoever this is you better be dying!"

"I feel like I am Gee Gee."

"Raven, where are you?" asked Gail.

"Lying on the floor in my Hummer. Come drink the rest of this fifth of Ciroc with me, I drank all of the Grey Goose."

"Raven you are going to give yourself liquor poisoning, who's with you?"

"My bodyguards Lance and Don, you know Gee Gee, you three are the only ones I can trust; out of the millions and millions of people on this earth, I can only trust three people. How sad is that?"

"Raven, give whomever is driving the phone please."

Gail heard rustling and Raven yelling slurred words away from the phone before hearing a soft baritone voice.

"This is Don."

"Don, this is Gail, Raven's therapist. Would you mind swinging by my house and picking me up? I think he and I need to talk."

She gave Don here address and told him to tell Raven that she'd see him in a little bit.

"Boss I'm going to get Gail she wants to talk to you," Says Don.

Raven snatches his phone and tosses it onto the seat, "Of course she does, she always wants to talk, just like a woman; talk... talk... talk... gosh."

When the Hummer pulled up in front of her home, she could hear Raven yelling at someone. She opens the door to see him lying on the floor with a vodka bottle tucked under his arm.

"Gee Gee! Come on in, have a seat." Raven says while patting the seat.

"Raven you want to explain to me what's going on with you? You advance to the Wimbledon finals only to get disqualified and fined seventy five thousand dollars for fighting on the premises and now I find you on the floor of your vehicle sloppy drunk, what's the problem?"

"The problem is Dale, I should've beat the hell out of that punk a long time ago. He deserved it, he asked for it."

"Raven no man deserves to be beat the way that you beat him you..."

"HE MADE HER ABORT MY CHILD! THAT WAS THE LAST AND FINAL THING I WAS GOING TO LET HIM STEAL FROM ME! HE TOOK THE LOVE OF MY LIFE AND HE TOOK MY SEED SO DON'T TELL ME HE DIDN'T DESERVE THAT ASS WHIPPING I GAVE HIM!"

"Besides Dale, who has stolen from you before and what did they steal?"

"No! No! We are not about to do this. This is not about my childhood, this is about Dale and his raggedy ass wife."

"So someone stole something from you when you were a child, what was it?"

Raven pulls himself up and stares at Gail.

"You are hard headed as hell, what did I just say? I'm not about to go into all of that. Hand me that cup on the side of you, I need another drink."

She takes the cup and holds it inches away from him.

"I'll give you this cup if you tell me who stole from you."

"Stop playing Gee Gee, Ugh, my step-father okay, my step-father stole from me."

He reaches for the cup and she snatches it away.

"What did he steal Raven?"

"MY MOTHER AND MY BROTHER GAIL! He sold my little brother Marlon for some heroin the garbage man found his body in a dumpster a few miles from where we lived three days later. After that my mother went crazy, she's in a mental ward right now as we speak. Now give me the cup Gail."

When he reaches for the cup she hugs him. He tries to push her away but she only squeezes tighter letting him know that she wasn't going to let go. He finally stops fighting and hugs her back.

"I miss him so much, I miss them both so much," he cries.

After a few minutes they finally broke their embrace. Raven hadn't really looked at Gail when she first got in but since there is a streetlight shining into the Hummer he could now see how much she's change physically. He could tell that she has gone from being thick to frail. Her eyes are baggy and she looked drained, she didn't look healthy. Her worried eyes begged him to open up more.

"He was three years old and I was five. He was such a happy boy, smiled and spoke to everyone he came across, he was special Gail. We couldn't even have an open casket he'd been beaten so bad, it was like he was tortured. Mama, she was never the same after that, she completely shut down mentally which caused for me to go into foster care. It seems like everything I love or could love gets taking away."

He sat next to Gail locking his arm in hers.

"I've confessed so much to you Gail, now it's your turn. I know you have pain, everyone does. Where is yours?"

She rested her head on his shoulder, "Raven soon none of that will even matter."

> *"Evil may not prevail in the end, but it certainly doesn't fail to devastate in its time."~ Richelle E. Goodrich*

~Gail~

Raven finally agreed to go home and get some rest around five a.m. Gail was exhausted and in pain, all she wanted to do was crawl under the covers and drift away. She enters her bedroom to see the light on her answering machine blinking. She presses play and hears a frantic Monroe.

"Gail its Monroe, Chaz is fighting for his life; he was in a car accident. They won't give anyone but his spouse and immediate family any information on his status. All I know is they moved him into Neuro-ICU. We're at Northwestern Memorial Hospital on Eerie St; hurry Gail."

She scoops up her keys and phone and bolts out the house. So many things were going through her mind like the last time she had seen Chaz, their last meeting was an emotional and surprising one, she'd never seen him vulnerable and desperate before and it was quite saddening. She was now starting to regret the way that she ended the email she sent him in response to his ultimatum.

It didn't take long for her to make it to the hospital and it didn't take her long to run into Monroe. She watch him pace nervously in front of the entrance doors before approaching him.

"Where is he Monroe?"

"All I know is that they moved him from the ER to Intensive Care. Since he doesn't have family here, they are only willing to disperse information to you; his wife. Look I'm going home, I can't handle all of this, and I was just waiting for you to get here."

Gail could hear the disgust in Monroe's voice when he said, "his wife." Instantly annoyed, she pushes past him and finds the front desk.

"Excuse me miss, my name is Gail Washington and I'm looking for my husband Chaz Washington, he was in a car accident."

"Oh yes here we go, he was in surgery and has been placed on the ninth floor in room nine thirty two. Go down that hall right there and make a left, you will find some elevators on the right hand side, here's a visitors pass."

Gail followed the directions given by the nurse and went up to the Neuro- ICU. She met with another nurse who paged for the surgeon that operated on Chaz.

"Mrs. Washington, hi I'm Dr. James Kohn, I'm the surgeon that operated on your husband."

"Hello Dr. Kohn how is he?"

"Let's have a seat over here, Mrs. Washington when the EMT's arrived at the scene of the crash his car was smashed against a tree upside down. There was no other car at the scene; he may have fallen asleep at the wheel or lost control trying to swerve from hitting an animal. The ambulance technicians brought him in and we immediately started CPR. He had massive head trauma and internal bleeding. We placed him in surgery where I made an incision to relieve the pressure on his brain caused by the blood build up from the crash. I thought it would make a difference but it hasn't. Even though we performed CPR, he was unresponsive. The brain begins to die six minutes after the heart stops. I'm sorry Mrs. Washington but your husband has no brain activity. I ordered a confirmatory test called Cerebral Blood Flow. This involves the injection of a mild radioactive isotope into the blood stream. By placing a radioactivity counter over the head, one can measure the amount of blood flow into the brain. The test takes twenty to thirty minutes to perform. If there is no blood flow to the brain as

demonstrated by this study, the brain is dead"
he explains.

"And, what were the results?" inquires
Gail.

"The test revealed that he is indeed
brain dead. But before we ran this test we ran
his blood for infections, and things of that sort
like we do before we use any diagnostic agent.
And we found something."

"Dr. Kohn please just spit it out, I'm
really not in the mood for all of these dramatic
pauses. Please, what is it?"

"Your husband is HIV positive, that
doesn't mean that you are but you should get
tested. I'm sorry."

It was like Gail was hit with a ton of bricks. It
all made sense now, she remembered Monroe
looking sick in Dr. Erickson's office and Chaz
looking ill when he came to see her at hers.
Looking up at the ceiling she silently asked
God why. She must have been deep off into
her thoughts because Dr. Kohn tapped her on
her knee to get her attention.

"Mrs. Washington hello, did you hear
me?"

"Yea... yea I'm sorry, what were you
saying?"

"I said that your husband is on life support but given the circumstances and the result of the cerebral blood flow test, I see no point in keeping him on the ventilator. Ultimately it's your decision, would you like to see him?"

Gail trailed behind Dr. Kohn to Chaz's room. She gasped at the sight of his bruised face and heavily wrapped head.

"He looks like not an ounce of life is within him" she says.

"I'll leave you two alone, if you have any more questions notify the nurse and she will get a hold of me okay?"

She ignores him and walks slowly over to her lifeless husband. She ran her fingers along his battered arm as she sat next to him.

"Oh Chaz... I don't know if I should be furious with you or sad." She plants a lingering kiss upon his bandaged forehead.

"Mrs. Washington, again I think you should get your blood ran to see if you're infected" he says.

"It truly doesn't matter Dr. Kohn..." she looks over at him, "I'm already as good as dead."

~Gail~ (Cont.)

It's been four days since Chaz was taken off of life support. He mentioned to her in the early years of their marriage that being buried freaked him out, so he wanted to be cremated. Along with her parents and Zaya, she said a prayer and poured his ashes into Lake Michigan, she hasn't left her bed since arriving home that day. She turned off her cell phone and unplugged her house phone but not before letting her loved ones know that she was going on hiatus indefinitely. All of this has made her realize two things for sure; she needs to put her plan into action and get those knuckle heads; Zaya, Raven, Nathaniel and Morgan to take interest in one another. Secondly, she needs to inform her clients of what's going on with her health, especially since she's decided to close the doors to the Healing Center for good. She was stinky and starving after going four days without bathing and only snacking on assorted nuts, raisins, cookies and chips. She showered and climbed back into bed with her laptop and a generous bowl of chicken noodle soup.

"First things first, if I'm going to throw a singles mixer I have to find a Venue. She called around to a few places when she finally decided on Sol Café, it has the intimate setting and the space she needs for this party. She's been there several times for meetings and it is perfect. After she secured the location, now she must pick up some games, wine and extra food.

"And invites, I'm going to invite all of my clients and associates who are single. By mouth and a reminder by email, it's only five days away, I hope they all will be able to make it." It occurred to her that she would need help if she wants this party to be a success. She instantly thought about her mother and how she had a good eye of who should be with whom; she told me not to marry Chaz and of course against her mother's better judgment she went to City Hall anyways.

"Hey mom are you busy?"

"Hey baby how are you feeling? You feeling okay? I've been worried about you Gail."

"I'm better mom, look I need your help. I've booked the Sol Café for the single mixer I want to throw. That place can hold about forty people comfortably, so I'm only inviting a select few. I have an idea of the menu and the entertainment that I will provide, there's one thing though, and all of this has to happen on this Thursday coming up."

"Gail that's five days from today, do you think people will show up on such short notice?" asked Mrs. Shannon.

"With hard work and prayer they will." She gave her mother a list of foods and wines that she would need for the party, she wrote herself a list of games, music selections and decorating ideas next she called Zaya.

"Oh my god Gail, I've been worried sick! I was giving you one more day on your hiatus and then I was coming over there."

"Yea yea, I need you to call my clientele and ask them to meet me at the office around four this afternoon. If they can't make it, tell them I will personally call them sometime next week and explain the reason behind me wanting to meet with them so abruptly.

"Okay sure Gail, no problem; but um, why do you want to meet with everyone?" questioned Zaya.

"Because... I have a huge announcement to make."

After Zaya called back and said that seventeen of her twenty-five clients have agreed to be at the Healing Center at four p.m. it left her only two and a half hours to get some things on her list for the mixer. She was pretty relaxed, she wasn't in any pain, Chaz's death still weighed on her heavy but she's never been the one to be low for too long. She met the owner of the Sol Café and they mapped out how the set will be for the mixer. She wrote him a check and thanked him for granting her the café on such short notice.

She arrived at her office feeling bittersweet; on one hand she feels a deep sadness for her decision to move on but then again, she also feels relieved that she won't have to suck up other people's sorrow. It just wouldn't be fair to them or to her to counsel them half-heartedly. She enters the sitting area greeted with a host of flowers, get well and sympathy cards from her clients. She went around the room giving hugs and thanks as they offer their condolences; Nathaniel even hugged her, which was surprising.

"Again thank you all for meeting me here on such short notice and for the thoughtful gifts; you all are truly appreciated and it's..."

She's interrupted by Nathaniel and Zaya bickering in the corner.

"Excuse me but what are you two fussing about?" questions Gail.

"I politely asked him to stop texting and to give you his undivided attention and he calls me bitter; which I am not!" explains Zaya.

"You are too!" Nathaniel sticks his tongue out at Zaya.

"Will you two stop it please? I have something I need to say."

"What's up Gee Gee, you leaving us or something?" inquired Raven.

Damn, of all of the things he could've said, he hit the nail right on the head

"Well since you asked, the answer to that is yes, I am retiring."

The entire room begins to shoot questions at her.

"Hold on everyone, please, I'll explain if you just quiet down." She sits on top of Zaya's desk, "I've listened to all of your problems, heartaches, failures, achievements, wishes and dreams; and now I need all you of you to just sit and listen to me right now."

"We're sorry Gail, what is it that you would like to say?" says one of her clients.

"Well before I tell you the bad news I have good news for you. I'm throwing a singles mixer on August twenty second; that's a Thursday. I would love for all of my singles in here to attend, it would mean the world to me. There will be food, drinks and entertainment. You will socialize for a couple of hours and then me and my matchmaker of a mother will send you on mini-dates with two individuals who you believe that you have the most chemistry with, of course we will voice our opinions but it will ultimately be your decision."

God I'm lying through my teeth because Zaya, Morgan, Nathaniel and Raven have no idea that this is a trap

"After the mini-dates you will choose the person that you feel you had the best chemistry with and with that person you will go on a real date that upcoming weekend. And that's not all, I will be providing the transportation courtesy of Windy City Limos. I can tell by the look on all of your faces you are wondering why I'm doing this and this is why, there has been a theme of some sort in my sessions with my singles that are in here. Some of you admit it and some of you are still struggling with the truth, but in your own words you all told me that you all are missing the same exact thing in your lives, and that's love. I mean look at you all, you have the looks, the careers and the perks gained from those careers but you're still not happy... you still feel empty. I want to help you because I love you, each of you. I promised myself that I would do some sort of good deed before I left this earth, and this is it." She slid down from the desk and faced Morgan, "I want to show you that it's okay to love despite a tragic lost." She glanced over at Nathaniel, "I want to prove that even though some of us grew up unloved, does not mean love doesn't exist." She walks over to Zaya, "I want you to understand that you are worth being loved, you deserve it." She looks over at Raven and tilts her head to the left, "I want to convince you that not everyone is the same, there is someone out there that will love you the way that you should be loved." She walks over to the window and leans against the glass, "So please do me this favor and show up to the mixer; like I said, it will mean a lot to me."

"Of course we will show up, anything for you Gail, right everybody?" says Morgan looking around the room.

Everyone verbally and nods in agreement with Morgan.

"So what's the bad news Gail, anything we can help you with?" asks another client.

"No Matt, no one can help me with this situation, it's pretty much set in stone." She sat on the coffee table with her head lowered, "I found out a couple of months ago that I'm dying; I'm in the final stages of cervical cancer and I chose not to seek treatment for it. Now before you all bombards me with questions I made the decision not to get treated for a reason. My entire life I've always done what everyone else has wanted me to do, I'm a people's pleaser. I've always tried to live up to other people's expectations, I put other people's wants and needs before my own. I want my last days to be full of love and good times, I feel I deserve that." She stood up and took a look around the room. "I know a lot of you, if not most of you thought that I had it all together, and I did not. My husband, may he rest in peace, was a chronic cheater. He has gave me several STD's which one of them is the cause of my cervical cancer..."

Several people gasped simultaneously, appalled at her confession.

"Oh my god," mumbles Nathaniel.

"As weird as this may be, I'm going to ask anyway, I don't want to only invite you to the mixer, and I would like you all to come to my funeral, if you will" says Gail.

"Okay I can't take this," Zaya says.

Raven walks over to Gail and hugs her, "I knew something wasn't quite right, you don't look the same, you've lost weight and you look exhausted all of the time now. Why didn't you tell us sooner?"

"Hey I know you, you're the tennis player that beat up some other tennis player and got kicked out of the tournament the other day" shouts Matt.

Raven pulls his hat lower on his head and sits back down.

"I didn't want to worry any of you, I care about you too much, but I realized that telling you was the right thing to do. I need to live and be happy, I want to be free of all responsibilities, that's why I've also decided to close the Healing Center down for good. Don't worry, I have colleagues that are just as good and I've already talked to them about taking you all on. Once again, it's ultimately up to you. Zaya there are even job offers for you if you are willing to accept them."

"So you just have everything all figured out huh Gail? You just waltz in here invite us to a party, tell us you're dying, invite us to your future funeral and then tell us that the one place with the one person that we can be ourselves with will no longer be available to us. Well that's just great Gail," says Matt.

"Matt, please try and understand that this is in all of our best interest, I am no good to any of you in the state that I'm in. It's not like the office is closing today. I plan on keeping it open the remainder of this month to mid-September, for all of you who are interested in setting up a final session with me."

The energy in the room is very low and Gail knows that it will take time for everyone to process what is happening.

"I love all of you and I hope that we can part on good terms, to my singles please sign the singles mixers invite on the yellow clipboard on Zaya's desk. Fill in your numbers and emails alongside your names. I will email you reminders and a flyer explaining the event, dress code, etc."

Gail watches them one by one sign their names, some more reluctant than others, she spots Nathaniel trying to sneak out.

"Dr. Thompson where do you think you're going? Get your tail in here and sign this clipboard. As a matter of fact, you, Raven, Zaya and Morgan get your asses over here."

"Gail please, look at me, I don't need to attend a mixer to meet women," says Nathaniel.

"Yea and I'm good looking, rich and famous, so you already know I don't need any help getting pus..."

"Raven you better not say it! And I don't want to hear it. All of you better be there Thursday night and I'm not joking, do I make myself clear?" says Gail.

"I'll be there," replies Morgan.

"Yea me too," Says Zaya.

"Ugh, yea I hear you," says Raven.

All four of them turn to look at Nathaniel.

"What, what the hell are y'all staring at me for?" asked Nathaniel.

Gail raises her eyebrow and folds her arms.

"Okay, aight, damn, I'll be there."

She holds out her arms and smiles, "Great, group hug!"

All of them rolled their eyes and left.

"Oh it's like that? Okay forget y'all too!"

"Guilt is the very nerve of sorrow."~
Horace Bushnell

~Mrs. Shannon~

For an entire hour Mr. Shannon watches his wife pace back and forth along their patio. She has been behaving differently since receiving the news about their daughter. Her laugh, her smile, even the way she walks has changed; she hasn't been the woman he's been married to for the past thirty plus years. She's always been a proud woman, but lately her head hangs in shame; soft sobs on the other side of the glass doors guides him out of thought and onto the patio.

"What's wrong Gillian?"

"Nothing honey, do you need something?"

"Gillian we've been together since we were teenagers, I know when something is bothering you; now what's the matter?" inquires Mr. Shannon.

"Marvin please..."

"Gail, what's... wrong?"

"My baby is letting herself die because of me!"

She ran into his arms crying uncontrollably.

"Sweetheart, why would you say a thing like that? You are a wonderful mother; you were tough on our children but it was for good reason. You taught them to never settle for less; to always strive to be the best. Because of you they are ambitious, driven, goal-oriented individuals. We did the best that we could with our children, we taught them right from wrong, now what they did when they went out into the world on their own is on them, not us."

She breaks their embrace and looks at him, "Are you serious right now Marvin? I was hard on Gail, not Monroe. Monroe got away with murder and you know it. Everything Gail did wasn't good enough, I just pushed and pushed. I made her work so hard for my approval, Marvin can you find me five pictures in our family photo album with Gail smiling in them? No you can't because I made her childhood and teenage years miserable. She was always studying, volunteering, and taking extra academic classes not because she liked it Marvin but because she wanted her mother to say four simple words; I'm proud of you. And I never did, I never told my little girl that I was proud of her. She never got to really live and I played a big part in that, so now she doesn't want to waste the little time she has left being doped up, weak and restricted; she just wants to live for once. And let's not talk about our son, never mind the fact that he's gay; that's actually the only thing that's not offensive about him. He's rude, lazy, vindictive, arrogant, selfish, self-centered and oblivious to the very fact that everything he touches turns to dust." She lifts her hands and cuffs her husband's face, "You can continue to pretend all that you want, like we did our best raising Gail and Monroe, but baby truth is; we messed up somewhere along the way and it has gone too far and on for far too long. I've never owed anybody anything my entire life, but I just realized that I owe Gail the love and support that I never gave her as a child. Marvin I can't let her go, not like this. I can't let her leave here feeling not good enough and unloved, I might not have much time to do it, but I'm about to be the mother I should've been a long time ago." She plants a kiss on his chin and walks away sobbing, leaving him alone to ponder her remorseful words.

"Great deeds are usually wrought with great risks."~ Herodotus

~The Hook-up~

Gail:

Gail created a love fest in passionate shades of dark reds that awaken the sense of desire, along with pinks creating a romantic spot to chill. She spent countless hours' googling different sites for these awesome ideas, and couldn't wait to use them! She filled large glass vases with feather boas and feather ticklers. All around the café were flickering candlelight with printed teasers like: "Tickle me", "Blame it on the Boa", "Flirt like you mean it" and "Dance with me." Her favorite was the cute idea to make it easier for the singles to meet by creating flirtatious name badges from blank buttons. Printed on the badges are catchy phrases like "For One Night Only I'll...", "Meet me, I'm..." "Will flirt for..." The singles will have to fill in the blanks and write his or her name with permanent markers. As she moved about the café she thanked God for a pain-free day so far, she felt great. The theme of the mixer is "Let's play" so she decorated the walls with twister sheets and monopoly boards. The guests will have to 'make their move' by collecting tokens from the other singles. She set up all of the other games like 'Nuts and Bolts' and 'Singles Bingo'.

"Hey mom, how is the food and drink set up looking?" asks Gail.

"I'm almost done, I've placed the ice buckets around the room along with the wine and cocktails; All I need to do now is place the trays of finger and interactive food in different areas of the café." Replies Mrs. Shannon!

"Interactive food?" questions Gail.

"Yea interactive food: food that they will have to put together themselves, like Tacos and Sundaes."

"Nicccceeeeee, and here I thought finger sandwiches and wraps would do the trick, good thinking mom!"

Gail gives her mother a kiss on the cheek and takes off to find the DJ.

"Remember turn up the volume for early guest, the music will feel the empty space and will keep them from feeling the party hasn't started yet. Once more partygoers show up turn the volume down, I don't want them to feel like they have to compete with the music. Oh and skip the slow jams, only up tempo beats, thanks DJ Play."

She looks around the café satisfied with the set up; it was sensual, engaging and inviting. All she needed now was for everyone to show up and be on their best behavior. She burst out in prayer at the thought of Raven, Zaya, Morgan and Nathaniel being on their best behavior. She retrieves her cell phone and begins text messaging them.

"Lord pretty please let this work."

Zaya:

Zaya was stepping out of the shower when she received a text message from Gail.

"Hey Zaya, I hope you are getting all dolled up for the mixer, remember: keep it classy not trashy. You know you sit your breast too high a nipple can pop out at any minute. See ya in an hour, love ya!"

"No she didn't come at me like that! Wait until I see her!"

Raven:

"Jasmine don't lick my chest girl, I don't want to smell like your saliva, I just took a shower." He grabs her bra off of the floor and uses it to wipe off his chest.

"Whatever, your phone is buzzing AGAIN!"

"What are you yelling for?! Give me my phone since it's buzzing AGAIN!"

"Get it yourself Rave." She snatches her bra out of his hand.

"What? You're standing right next to it! Get your trifling ass out of my house!"

"Yea whatever, what would you like for dinner?" she asks as she hands him the phone.

"Fried chicken, macaroni and cheese and some mixed vegetables; thank you baby."

She gives him the finger and walks out. He checks his phone to see that it's a text from Gail, he hesitated a bit before opening the message.

"Shit I forgot about tonight, she's probably cursing me out in the message."

"Hey Raven! I hope you're getting so fresh and so clean for tonight. Don't forget the dress code: no jeans, hoodies, gym shoes, hats or sweaters. I need you to come in your grown man attire. See you in an hour!"

"I can't wear a fitted hat? Oh hell naw, these chicks better be model chicks, they better be bad!"

Nathaniel:

"Son, shouldn't you be getting ready to go to Gail's party tonight?"

"Yea I don't know dad, I mean I don't need help getting a woman."

"No you don't, you just need help on how to keep a woman."

"Dad don't start with me, wait hold on for a minute, someone just text me."

He looks at his phone and sees a message notification from Gail.

"It's a text from Gail."

"Well what does it say?" asks Mr. Thompson.

It says, *"Nate you better bring your ass or else I'm coming to get you and if I have to come and get you, you're going to be in big trouble and I'm serious! Now throw on your Armani suit and be here in an hour, Capiche?"*

"This lady is crazy, I should've never gone to her office that day."

Laughing Mr. Thompson began to tease his son, "You better get dressed son before you get in trouble."

Morgan:

"Damn I can't decide on this black great glam dress or this pink Betsy Johnson dress; ugh! I hate parties... I hate dating... Lord why am I stressing about this? You know what, I'ma call my mama, she will know which dress I should wear."

Just as she was about to dial her mother's number a text from Gail interrupted her.

Hey Morgan! I think you should wear your hair up tonight, you have such a pretty face. I don't have to say dress classy because you're the queen at that. I know whatever you choose you will look stunning in it, see you in an hour!

Zaya:

Zaya walks in and is immediately greeted by Gail's mother.

"Good evening Zaya, welcome to the 'Let's play' singles mixer, choose a name badge and a permanent marker, fill in the blank and write your name." instructs Mrs. Shannon.

"Hey Mrs. Shannon, I think I'll take this one here, this place looks great! Gail did her thing up in here."

"She sure did! Here is a screw for the nuts and bolts game we will play later so hold on to that. There's food, drinks and fun icebreakers for you to dabble in. Go find Gail, she'll introduce you to the other guests, and girl it's some fine young men in here."

Laughing, Zaya hugs Mrs. Shannon, "I'm sure there are Mrs. Shannon."

Gail:

Gail sneaks up behind the two while they're hugging and tickles Zaya.

"Hey girlie you look beautiful! Glad that you could make it." Gail says while embracing Zaya.

"Thanks for the invite, I was telling your mom how great it looks in here."

"Thanks now enough chit-chatting with me, let me introduce you to some men."

Gail and her mother has strategically mapped out who Zaya, Morgan, Nathaniel and Raven will talk to first before setting them up with each other. She spots Malcolm talking with some of the other men by the DJ station and approaches the group with Zaya.

"Zaya I'd like for you to meet Malcolm West, he models for Calvin Klein and Sean John. Malcolm, why don't you take Zaya to get a drink?"

"Well I don't mind if I do." Malcolm says holding his arm out for Zaya to grasp.

"Great now you two go have some fun."

"Hey Gail what's up? The DJ jamming up in here, this is my jam!"

Gail spins around to see Morgan in a black drape neckline dress with open shoulder sleeves, dancing to 'Hot Thang' by Talib Kweli, she looks radiant.

"Morgan you look gorgeous! Turn around let me see the back, girl this dress is fierce!"

Morgan twirls around and poses, "Well thank you girl, thank you. I love the décor Gail and some of the center pieces."

"Center pieces?" Gail glances in the direction Morgan's staring and realizes what she's talking about.

"It's funny that you're interested in him because I actually picked him out for you, let me introduce you two."

"Wait Gail wait, is there anything in my teeth?" Morgan gave Gail a kool-aid smile.

"Chile you're fine, now come on."

Jarrod was making himself a cocktail when his colleague walks over with one of the most beautiful women he's ever seen.

"Jarrod this is Morgan, Morgan this is Jarrod."

Jarrod offers his hand, "Hi Morgan."

She accepts his hand and shakes it "Hi Jarrod."

"Jarrod is a Criminal Psychologist. We attended the same master's program, how about you two go try some of my veggie wraps."

"I'm not a vegetarian," says Morgan.

Gail pinches her on the arm, "Just go over there and try some."

Rubbing her arm Morgan follows Jarrod across the room. Gail shakes her head and finds the DJ.

"Hey Play, could you lower the music I need to make an announcement"

"Sure thing Gail" he replies.

"Hey everyone, can I have your attention for a brief second please. A lot of you know me and a few of you don't. My name is Gail Washington and I'm responsible for this singles mixer tonight. I would just like to thank you all for coming out and looking quite fabulous may I add. Now that you've had a chance to..."

"Gee Gee, I know you're not starting the fun without me are you?"

"Ladies and Gentlemen Raven Rob..." Gail was cut off by a female guest

"Oh we know who he is, he's Raven Robinson the richest tennis athlete in the world and well-known bachelor." She walks up to him and runs her finger down his chest, "You look even more handsome in person Mr. Robinson."

"Well thank you baby, why don't you come find me a little bit later and we'll talk." He replies.

"Um excuse me, this is no place for groupies, so you missy, what's your name tag say? Claudia? Yea you can leave, mom can you see this young lady out for me please?"

Mrs. Shannon walks Claudia to the entrance and thanks her for coming.

"Damn Gee Gee, why are you hating on me like that?!" questions Raven.

Gail rolls her eyes and turns back towards the crowd, "Anyway, like I was saying before I was rudely interrupted. Now that you all have had a chance to get acquainted a little bit, it's time to kick off our first game. Mom would you like to explain the activity while I pass out the game cards."

"Hello I'm Mrs. Shannon; Gail's mom, and the first game of the night is singles bingo. With singles bingo each of you will receive a game card with interesting facts about the other singles. The object of the game is to find the person who fits the description on the board. The first person to get bingo will win a complimentary gift, you have thirty minutes. Does everyone have a bingo card? If you do not, raise your hand and Gail will give you one."

Everyone hands remained down so she started the clock.

"Okay you guys, TIME... STARTS...
NOW!" yells Mrs. Shannon.

Nathaniel:

It was like he had walked into a mad
house. There were men and women frantically
moving around the café with cards and pens
like a group of hungry journalist.

"I see you did the smart thing and
showed up."

He spun around to see Zaya in a way that he's
never seen her before, he actually thought
that she was sexy.

"Aye don't sneak up on me like that,
shouldn't you be running around like a chicken
with their head cut off like the rest of these
folks?" he says.

"Whatever Thompson, just get your bolt
from Mrs. Shannon over there and a bingo
card from Gail." says Zaya.

"What if I don't want to?"

"Oh you don't want to, okay hold on."
Zaya goes up to DJ Play and asks him if she
could use his microphone for a brief second.

"Zaya, what are you doing?!" Nathaniel shouts.

"Mic check one, two, one, and two. Gail, Nathaniel says he doesn't want to play any of your stupid games and that the only reason why he came was to see how many numbers he could fill up his little black book with!" yells Zaya.

The entire room turns towards Nathaniel and stares, Gail instantly began to massage her temples.

"No, she's lying! I didn't say that! Zaya you wanna play? Okay, I got you!"

Zaya sticks her tongue out at him before rejoining the party.

"Nathaniel, what is wrong with you and Zaya?" ask Gail.

"She wants me, that's what it is Gail."

"And what about you, do you want her?"

The confused look on his face and his silence tells Gail that he does.

Yes, this match should be easy. They want each other but is just too stubborn to admit it.

"Here this is a screw, you'll need it for our next game so don't lose it let's go meet some women." Says Gail.

Gail:

"Okay mom they're all here and having a good time eating, drinking and dancing. Now did you remember to give them the matching screws and bolts? Raven's screw matches Morgan's bolt and Zaya's to Nathaniel's right?"

"Yes honey everything is going as planned, are you sure about Zaya and Nathaniel? They fight like cats and dogs."

"Yes I'm very sure about those two, they are perfect for each other. Now let's kick off the next game, DJ Play, microphone please."

"Excuse me ladies and gentlemen; hi it's me again, since no one has gotten bingo we're going to move on to a different game. This game is called nuts and bolts, Mrs. Shannon gave every man a screw and every woman a bolt. The object of the game is to find your match; you will have to go around testing everyone's out in order to find the matching piece. The man or woman with the matching piece is the man or woman you will go on your mini-date with. Once again you will only have a half hour to complete the task, good luck, time... starts... now!"

Gail doesn't know if it's the liquor or if it's the fact that men get to try and 'screw' something, but everyone is really into this one. She observes damn near every woman in the room waiting in line to see if their bolt is a match to Raven's screw. Gail peep's Nathaniel flirting with one of the few women who weren't throwing themselves at her celebrity client. Morgan and Zaya are working feverishly to find their matches, you can see the disappointment on their faces when they realize their bolt doesn't fit.

Gail grabs the microphone, "Fifteen minutes left everyone!"

"We have a match!" yells Clyde and Helen, who are also old classmates of Gail's.

"Hey! Alright we have a match, congratulations, please see Mrs. Shannon for further instructions. Come on guys let's get those matches!" says Gail.

Morgan:

She didn't want to seem thirsty like the other chicks here tonight so she waited until there was no longer a line to meet him, he was fine though. He's chocolate with a wide back and broad shoulders, and his eyes can wet every pair of panties in the room, they are so seductive.

"Excuse me Raven, I don't know if you remember me, but I was there that day we all met at Gail's office."

"Oh yea, Morgan how are you?"

"I'm good, it's only a few minutes left in the game and I realized I haven't tried to see if your screw matches my bolt." She raises her hand to meet his and places the bolt on the tip and began to screw it on.

"Well look at that, it fits" says Morgan.

"Yea, we're a match." He says gazing into her eyes.

Lord Jesus if this man doesn't stop looking at me like that, things are going to get X-rated real quick.

Gail sees that Morgan and Raven match their parts together.

"We have another match, Raven and Morgan ladies and gentleman, only five minutes left, make your move!" Gail shouts.

Gail:

She looks for Zaya and sees her stuffing her face with tacos.

"Zaya what are you doing? Go find your match." Says Gail.

"I tried, I don't think my bolt has a match" replies Zaya.

"So you're saying that you've tried every man in this café? Did you try Nathaniel?"

"Hell no and I'm not either."

Gail pulls Zaya from the snack table across the room to Nathaniel.

"Um excuse me Paula but I need to see Nathaniel for a minute."

"What's up Gail? I was trying to take that home" says Nathaniel.

"Yea no thank you to that, this is not that type of party, have you two tried to see if your parts match?"

"NO!" Zaya and Nathaniel said simultaneously.

"Well you need to, there is only two minutes left in the game, come on now." Gail says.

Nathaniel and Zaya both look at each other and roll their eyes. He walks up to her and holds his piece out.

"Come on, let's get this over with." he says.

She takes her bolt and begin to work it down, both immediately in shock that their pieces fit together.

"Oh you have got to be kidding me," said Zaya.

"Times up everyone! Does everyone have a match? Yes? Ok great, gather around to hear what's happening next."

The crowd gravitated towards the center of the room where Gail was to share what was next on the agenda.

"So like it was explained before the game started, you and your match will go on a mini-date. You will spend fifteen minutes with that person to learn about them, but there's a twist; not only will you have a mini-date with your screw and bolt match, but you will get to have a mini-date with a person you personally choose for yourselves. You will also spend fifteen minutes with them. Wait a minute, there's another twist; at the end of both mini-dates not you but Mrs. Shannon and I will pick who you will go on your master date with. Of course that decision will be made after we've spoken with you and have gotten your opinions on the dates. Your first date will be with the person who you choose and your second mini-date will be with nuts and bolts match. Okay everyone let's start dating!"

Raven:

Raven picked Donna for his first mini-date. She was a thick Latina with a set of double D's which commanded attention, yea he plans on taking her home tonight.

"Raven Robinson, reigning men's tennis champ, well up until recently. What is a fine, wealthy man like you doing here?" asks Donna.

Leaning in he whispers, "Well baby, I'm not above meeting women on humbler grounds instead of celebrity parties and fundraisers."

"You are so Haannddsooommme."

He thought he was about to faint, her breath smelled like a backed up sewer drain.

"Shit! Damn! Um."

"What's wrong baby, you okay?" she asked.

Raven slid to the other side of the booth with his fist covering his nose.

"No I'm not, your mouth has just upset all of my insides, and my got damn stomach is turning. God you need to see a doctor about that, you just offended the hell out of me. I don't have to take this kind of abuse, deuces!" He leaves her popping a handful of icebreakers in her mouth.

Zaya:

"So Malcolm, how long have you been a model?"

"I've been modeling for ten years now, I started out at the tender age of fourteen."

Zaya did a double take, "Wait a minute, you started modeling ten years ago when you were fourteen years old; that will make you twenty-four!"

"Yea it would, is that a problem?"

"Hell yea that's a problem, your young ass can't do anything for me but get me pregnant and look good on my arm, that's it!" she says.

"Look baby age is nothing but a number. I'll have my own place and car soon; it's just hard to leave my mother! She does everything for me, not sure if I'd ever find a woman to come close to her."

This fool is not only a Gerber baby but he's a mama's boy, oh hell no, time to go!

"You know what sweetie, I'm going to go on ahead and wish you a good night because this right here is not going to work. I can't date a guy whose old school music is Nivea and Bone Thugs-N-Harmony, I'm sorry can't do it, take care."

"Wait a minute, you're just going to leave me like that?"

"Yes I am, now if you will excuse me. I need to find Gail and backhand her in the face."

Nathaniel:

"So Paula, tell me about yourself, what do you do for a living?"

"I'm a mortician."

"A mortician, that's different! Why was that your choice of a career?"

"It started when I was a child, most children are afraid of dead bodies but I wasn't. When I found my grandmother dead in the bath tub I wasn't alarmed, I actually washed her hair before calling for help. It's just something about the look of a dead person, it's very interesting."

Nathaniel chokes on his wine, "Well that's um, that's um, very um..."

"Odd? Yea I know, but I've always been sort of different you know? I'd find dead animals around the small town I grew up in and I'd bury them in my backyard. There must be about a hundred dead animals in my parents' backyard. Rabbits, cats, squirrels, even the ones that were road kill, I gave them all a funeral. Yep I love what I do, what else would you like to know?"

"Nothing, nothing at all! I know all that I need to know, excuse me."

"Where are you going, and what is it that you know?" she asked.

"Seriously, you're really asking me that question? Your ass is crazy! A straight lunatic! Ugh! Where is Gail?!"

Morgan:

"Morgan I must say that you are drop dead gorgeous, you are definitely a treasure."

"That's so sweet Jarrod, thank you. So tell me more about you."

"Well as you know I'm a criminal psychologist, the most boring job in the world. I'm an Aries, I love Italian food, pretty women and..."

"YOU LOVE TO LIE AND CHEAT ON YOUR WIFE!"

Morgan looks behind Jarrod to see a woman with her belly hanging over her too little shorts like a popped can of biscuits, black as tar with a blonde tangled weave.

"Bookie what the hell are you doing here? You've been following me again?!"

"Yea I've been following you, I wanna see what's stopping you from coming home Jarrod! Who is this bitch?!"

"Hold on baby, watch your mouth. I'll beat your ass back into the zoo that you came from King Kong." Says Morgan.

"No this bitch didn't! Jarrod you're gonna just let her talk to me that?! I'm your wife!"

"Well hell Bookie, it's not like she's lying."

"Jarrod bring your trifling ass on! Let's go!" She grabs him by the ear and forces him to stand up.

"Yo Morgan, can I still call you sometimes?" he yells.

"Hell naw! What the hell do you think this is?!"

Morgan storms off in search of Gail.

Gail:

"HOLD ON! WAIT A MINUTE! We can all sing together but we can't all talk at the same time. Now Raven, you were saying?"

"Gail that got damn girl melted my damn insides with her halitosis ass mouth. I've never felt so violated in my life! My stomach will never be the same Gail!" says Raven.

"Man please I would've took her over the chick I had. I was on a date with the angel of death, she gets her rocks off collecting dead animals and shit. All I could think about was pet cemetery," says Nathaniel.

"Yo Gail that's messed up, you're bogus for that one" Raven says laughing.

"That's nothing, Gail almost got me locked up for statutory rape, that damn boy is under twenty-five! Still living at home with his mama and driving her car! What were you thinking inviting him?" says Zaya.

"Gail! Gail! I need to talk to you!"

Everyone turns around to see Morgan storming their way.

"Yes Morgan, what is it?" asks Gail.

"He has a got damn wife Gail! I just almost cut her ass because she called me a bitch!"

"Morgan I had no idea Jarrod was married, he never told me!"

"Well he is and that broad looks like she was an extra in Planet of the Apes!"

"Okay you four just calm down, besides, it's time for your second mini-dates." Gail says smiling.

They all look at each other and shake their heads.

"Attention everyone, it is time for your second mini-date. Find that person and a comfy spot and start chatting!" instructs Gail.

Raven and Morgan:

"First things first, if I sit close to you, will the smell of your mouth send me to the upper room?"

"If I ask you to tell me about yourself, will your pet for a wife interrupt our date?"

"No, I'm single." He replies.

"No, I maintain good hygiene," she says.

"Tell me, what is it that you do?"

"I own a top scale salon called 'In Hair' on the north side of Chicago."

"A business woman, I like that; any children?"

"Nope not yet, how about you?"

"No kids for me either, do you know how to cook?"

"Yep, I was raised by my grandmother who is from Mississippi so I know how to cook all of that good southern food. Enough about me, I want to know how does it feel to be a celebrity."

"It has its pros and cons, more pros than cons so I can't complain."

Lord there he goes looking at me like that again, I don't know how long I can keep my legs tightly crossed like this.

"Let me get a bit deeper, why did you beat down that tennis player? You beat him like he stole something."

He did.

"You know, I don't want to talk about that, let's continue to keep the mood light. Let me ask you something, why is a beautiful woman like you single? I'm sure you have many suitors."

"You would think so huh, but I don't. I just haven't found someone worth my time ya know?" she says.

"Well maybe I can change that."

Zaya and Nathaniel:

"So what do you want to know pimpin?"

"Zaya who in the hell is pimpin? My name is Nathaniel, Dr. Thompson to you."

"Chile please you heard me, what do you want to know?"

"Okay I want to know why are you so bitter. Wait I can answer that for you. You fell for a man that you knew from the beginning was a piece of trash but still you chose to give your all to him and he cheated. He had outside kids on you and kids prior to you that he never told you about. He gave you STD's, spent all of your money and ate all of your food. Yea you look like the type with a ghetto story like that."

"You know what Thompson let's talk about you and why you treat women like crap. I'm guessing you have mommy issues, yea it's deeper than a high school heartbreak or a college love gone wrong" Zaya says.

"Chick you don't know anything about me."

"And I don't want to either, I'm out of here."

"We both know what the problem is Zaya."

"And what's that Nathaniel?"

"You're attracted to me but you know that you don't have a chance with a man like me, you are nowhere on my level."

"Now that's something that we can agree on, I'm above your level chump."

Gail:

"Time! Everyone come up to the front of the café please!" yells Gail.

She waits until she see's everyone before continuing.

"I would like to thank all of you for coming out tonight, you all have made my first singles mixer a success. To show my appreciation I will be gifting each of you a bottle of my favorite wine, a wine my husband Chaz use to love as well; Kistler Pinot Noir. Mom would you please hand out the gift bags to everyone. Also as promised, I have rented limos from Windy City limos for everyone's master date. Just sign your name under the dates and times that you think you will have your dates so I can call the company and set everything up. The only dates available are tomorrow and Saturday. Get your gift bags courtesy of me, sign up for your limo service and get the hell out! Thanks again everybody!"

Everyone signs their names except Zaya and Nathaniel.

"Guys, why aren't you signing up?" asks Gail.

"Because he's afraid of me." answers Zaya.

"Is that a challenge? And for your information I'm not afraid of you, you're just annoying" says Nathaniel.

Nathaniel walks up to Gail and snatches the sign-up sheet and signs his name.

"I'm up for the challenge, are you?"

Zaya takes the paper and signs her name next to his and walks out.

"Gail you know this is some bullshit don't you?" Nathaniel shakes his head as he exits the café.

"Oh Nate, you'll thank me later, you all will."

"The walls we build around us to keep sadness out also keeps out the joy."~ Jim Rohn

~Love Connection?

~

Nathaniel & Zaya

Zaya:

Zaya slid into a black stimulating dress with metallic highlights that shimmer with every sway of her hips. With the drape neckline and sultry cut out back; a pair of high heeled gold metallic pumps completes this sexy style. She decides to pull her hair into a Mohawk in the front and create a bun in the back. As she's slow dancing and singing Jill Scott's "Crown Royal' that's softly playing, she applies her make-up and sprays on her favorite fragrance 'Heartbreaker' by Victoria's Secret.

"Your hands on my hips pull me right back to you

I catch that thrust, give it right back to you

You're in so deep, I'm breathing for you

You grab my braids; arch my back high for you..." She's interrupted by her ringing cellphone, it's Nathaniel.

Damn it would be him to kill my vibe

"Hello?'

"The driver is almost there, be downstairs in five minutes."

"Um hello to you too Nathaniel and okay, downstairs in five, got it."

Click!

"Did this ignorant fool just hang up on me? Yes he did! Wait until I get into that limo!"

Nathaniel:

"Sir, shouldn't you get out and open the door for your date?" says the driver.

"My occupation is head pediatric surgeon at Rush Children's Hospital, I heal and save the youth, opening doors for women is not in my job description, it's in yours." replies Nathaniel.

The driver shakes his head and gets out of the limousine to open the door for Zaya.

"Good evening ma'am, my name is Austin and I'll be your chauffer for the night."

"Thank you for opening my door Austin, nice to meet you, I'm Zaya."

Zaya enters the limousine and is completely ignored by Nathaniel, she's had enough.

"Thompson what is your problem? First you hang up on me and now you don't even acknowledge me when I get into the limousine. Look we both agreed to do this for Gail, can't we just get along for a few hours? I mean are you at least going to tell me what we're doing tonight?"

"I'll think about it," he responds.

"I really wanna punch you in your eye sometimes Thompson, like really."

The Date:

After getting off to such a negative start, Zaya was second guessing going out with him. She loves Gail, but he seems bent on insulting her and he had one more time to do so and she was going to reach out and touch his face really hard. They rode to their mystery destination in silence, well it was a mystery to her because he hasn't said one word to her since his smart-aleck "I'll think about it" comment.

"We've arrived at the Signature Room, I'll be parked nearby waiting to drive you to your next destination," says Austin.

Austin opens the curb side door and helps Zaya get out of the limo.

"Thank you Austin, you're quite the gentleman, unlike some people I know."

He turns to tell her to 'kiss his ass' but at that exact moment he realized how beautiful she was. The dress she wore clinched her curves just enough to peek a man's interest but not so much to turn him off. Her lips look full and soft like Angelina Jolie's and her legs look like they belong to Tina Turner.

"Are we going to eat or are you going to stare at me all night?" asks Zaya.

"Man do you ever be quiet? Come on let's go."

When the elevator doors opened on the ninety fifth floors, Zaya is taken aback by the breathtaking view of the Chicago skyline.

"I've never been here before, this is beautiful."

"Of course you've never been here, you can't afford it."

Zaya shot him a look that would kill. They were given menus and seated at a candlelit table in the center of the room, allowing them to enjoy the spectacular view of the city.

"Order whatever you like; I know this is probably the first and last time you'll ever eat this good," says Nathaniel.

"Say another ignorant ass thing to me and watch I set it off up in this joint, stop disrespecting me Thompson!"

"Ooooo I'm scared, pipe down and choose an entrée, the waiter is on his way to our table."

"Hello my name is Troy and I'll be your server this evening, are we ready to order?"

"Yes I'll have the sautéed Scottish Salmon," answers Nathaniel.

"And you ma'am?" asks the waiter.

"I'll have the twin lobster tails."

"And any cocktails or wine to go with your meals?" the waiter asked.

"We'll have a bottle of Cabernet Sauvignon, thank you."

"And would you like that bottle of wine now or with your entrees?"

"Now." They said simultaneously.

"Okay that's a sautéed Scottish salmon and a twin lobster tail with a bottle of Cabernet Sauvignon; I'll take the menus and I'll be right back with your wine."

Zaya waits for the waiter to stroll off before addressing Nathaniel.

"Let's say something nice to each other, I'll go first, you look very handsome tonight Nathaniel."

"I only wear the best."

"So damn immodest, why can't you just say thank you?" Zaya asks.

"Why would I tell you thank you for something that I already know?" he replies.

"This was a bad idea."

"You think?" Nathaniel says.

They mean mugged each other the entire time the waiter poured wine into their glasses, picking up on the tension between the two, Troy made his presence brief.

"I'll sit this here to chill and I'll be back with your entrees."

Nathaniel thanks Troy and returns his gaze back to his date from hell.

"Okay, you want to play nice... let's do it. Um let's see here, what could I possibly say positive about you, hm. Ah! Okay! I have something, nice dress you have on there, it fits you well."

Zaya downs her entire glass of wine and quickly pours herself another glass. He was really trying her patience and she did not want to set it off in this prestigious establishment. All she can think about is how Gail owes her big time, sick or not, Gail was going to pay for this.

"You killed your glass of wine... thirsty?" he smugly asked.

Just as she was about to respond, Troy returns to the table with their entrees.

"The sautéed salmon for you sir and for you ma'am the twin lobster tails, Bon appetite!"

The two of them ate in silence, focusing solely on their meals. Nathaniel finishes first and waves down the waiter.

"Yes Troy I'm ready for the check, thanks."

"Nathaniel I'm not done eating." She looks up at him.

"So, ask for a box. We have one more thing to do and then you can go your way and I can go mines."

At this point she's on fire, "Fuck you Nathaniel! Fuck you and fuck this date! I love Gail but I refuse to spend another second with your arrogant, disrespectful, sexist ass! For some freaking reason you get your rocks off hurting, demeaning and degrading woman; well since you are making me pay for past sins committed against you let me apologize. I'm apologizing for whoever she is that did this to you. You hear me Nathaniel? I am saying that I am so sorry for whatever pain and heartache some woman or women has put you through. But know this; I love myself too damn much and I know that I'm not only a good woman but I'm a pretty awesome human being and I'll be damned if I let a man who doesn't know me from shit, continue to beat me down with ugly words; you may be handsome on the outside but on the inside you are cold and dark. Just like you didn't deserve the ugliness you were subjected to, I don't deserve it either and I am not going to take it; have a good night

Nathaniel... I'm done." She snatches up her clutch purse and rushes to the elevator. Nathaniel waves good bye to her and laughs coolly at her outburst. He wasn't aware of how bad he'd hurt her until she steps into the elevator and turns to face him, that's when he sees the tears streaming down her face.

~Love Connection~
(cont)

Raven & Morgan

Raven:

Raven looks himself over in his floor length mirror and admires what he sees. Whenever he had an event to attend, his tennis coach would always remind him, "Rave, a man makes the suit; the suit does not make the man" and he was most definitely wearing the hell out of this Joseph Abboud Pinstripe suit. He was having a hard time choosing a tie, so he held both ties against his chest to help with his decision.

"Rave the limo is here," Jasmine says rolling her eyes.

"What's the reason for your attitude Jazz? I'm with different women all of the time, hell damn near every threesome I've had you've been a part of so what's your problem?" he asked.

"I know that Raven but this time seems different, it just feels different." she says.

He stopped in the middle of tying his tie to stare at her in the mirror, narrowing his eyes, he spoke softly.

"See the problem is you've gotten too comfortable in my home. You've caught feelings for me when I made it very clear from day one to check your feelings at the door."

"Maybe... maybe not." she replies.

He applies some cologne and slides on his suit jacket. He walks over to her and kisses her on the cheek.

"Wrong answer, get it together or get your shit together and move on, understand?"

Jasmine nods her head yes and makes it up in her mind right then and there that a change has to be made.

Morgan:

Morgan had it all planned out. She purposely dressed to entice; her outfit of choice is a dress called 'Players club'. Its sassy cut outs create a visually distracting style sure to lure him in. Raven is fine, famous and has fortune and she wasn't about to let him slip through her fingers. As she sat in the limo waiting on her date, she pushes her breast up to her chin and checks her make-up in her compact mirror. When their driver Donte stepped out of the limo she knew that Raven was approaching.

"Whew girl, calm your nerves, you've caught ballers before, he's no different; you got this." She smiles at herself in the mirror before returning it back into her clutch purse.

When Donte opened the door and she sees Raven her mouth instantly dropped.

Damn he looks good as hell in that suit! Oooo weeee!

"What's up Morgan? You look like you've just seen the finest thing that you have ever seen in your life, well you have."

"Maybe I have, maybe I haven't, and I'll let you know. So where are we go..." she was cut off by the driver

"Yo Mr. Robinson, I'm a huge fan of yours! I've seen every single tournament that you've played in. My boys and I always talk about how we're happy that one of our own is dominating men's tennis, hell we usually only watch it to see Serena Williams wear those tight cat suits!"

Raven laughs, "Thanks man, and yea, she does wear the hell out of those cat suits."

"Maaaannn I'd knock the lining out of that coochie, straight up. You are really an inspiration man, the only thing I don't like is how a lot of society doesn't allow celebrities to be human beings. I wasn't mad at all when you beat the fear of God into Dale Trent. I can't stand his uppity ass; I am mad that you lost a few of your endorsements because of it."

"I'll be alright; the devil can't throw shade on my shine you feel me?"

"You must have a healthy amount of money stashed away if losing two of your biggest endorsements doesn't faze you," Morgan says.

"You've been reading up on me huh? Well I learned a long time ago to never spend more money than you make. And besides my career isn't over, I'm just on time-out for not playing nice on the playground with my friend."

Now Morgan was not only attracted to him physically and financially, she was digging his smooth persona; even the way he sits turns her on.

Yep, I most definitely have to have him.

The Date:

Raven made reservations at the 'Sixteen' restaurant inside of Trump Tower, he also reserved the 'Bridges Room' which is one of the private dining areas inside of the Sixteen. Once they were seated Morgan took a good look around the room.

Yea I've dated ballers and have dined in some upscale restaurants, but never privately; a girl can really get use to this.

They talked effortlessly over dinner, laughing and making jokes about one another's crazy high school and college stories.

"Hey, would you like to go to the bar section of the restaurant and continue or conversation?" asks Raven.

"Yes, I would like that, let me stop in the ladies room and freshen up a bit before we go."

Morgan rushed to the ladies' bathroom to finally answer Nikki's text, she's been blowing her phone up the entire date. She knows she shouldn't have told her receptionist who she was going out with tonight but she was excited to be out and about with one of the top black athletes in the world. She went inside of a stall and called Nikki.

"Nikki what's up girl? If you hear the sound of water that's me peeing, yes we're still here at the restaurant, dinner was awesome, and he is really charming. Girl yea! You know he's fine as hell! Girl those eyes of his are panty droppers, I swear I just wanna sit on his face. Oh he made reservations for us at the 'Sixteen Restaurant' inside of the Trump Towers. I know right! He has that mullah! Girl don't you worry, you already know me; I plan on popping this punany on him real soon so I can get that black American express card. What, feelings? Girl bye, you know only one man that tied me down and he's dead, I'm not going there again. Okay girl I'll call you hopefully in the morning and tell you about the second half of our date, bye." Morgan walks out the stall to the sink to wash her hands, she's startled when one of the waitresses starts washing her hands in the sink next to hers.

"Oh I'm sorry, I didn't know someone else was in here, I was all loud on the phone." says Morgan.

"Oh you're good, I thought you left though because I saw him walk out."

"Walk out? What?!" Morgan ran out of the bathroom to the front to ask their waiter have he seen Raven.

"As a matter of fact I did, he left with another young lady, and he told me to tell you that he had a great time and he hope you two can do it again." Said the waiter.

Morgan made it outside just in time to see Raven and a female getting inside of a Hummer truck.

"Raven I should cluck you in your forehead! Are you really leaving with another chick on our date?" screams Morgan.

"Sorry Morgan, I seen an old piece of ass of mines and I had flashbacks of what she use to do to me behind closed doors and right now, I want her to do it again. It's nothing personal, I'll call you."

"You just think that you can just handle me like all the rest of the little sluts you bang on a regular basis? Well you can't, I am not a whore." Morgan says.

"Oh but aren't you? Baby I can smell a gold digger from a hundred miles away. From the first time you saw me you set out to make me your newest come up, and from how smooth you are, you're a veteran at this shit so please spare me the dramatics. How many professional athletes, attorneys, doctors, and business men have you weaseled your way into their accounts? I know for a fact that I'm not your first target, am I Morgan. Take those alphabet undies off and put on your grown woman panties and accept the fact that I saw right through your bullshit. Have a great night Morgan, and oh you might want to tighten up your game before you hunt down your next victim."

Raven left Morgan in front of the hotel hurt and flabbergasted.

"There is enough heartache and sorrow in this life without our adding to it through our own stubbornness, bitterness, and resentment." ~ Dieter F. Uchdorf

~Gail~

"Zaya he said what?!" Gail invited Zaya over for appetizers and wine so she could get the scoop on her and Nathaniel's date the other night.

"Yep and then he says, 'Why would I tell you thank you for something that I already know?' Gail you know I was heated! I was livid! I wanted to Ike Turner his ass!" says Zaya.

"Girl I know that's right and what happened after that?" asked Gail.

"After that he decides that he's done eating and asks for the check and I'm like Nathaniel I am not finished eating. This fool tells me so and to get a box, that's when I lost it. I love you and I get what you're trying to do but honey that man doesn't need a wife, he needs Jesus."

"Well I'm so sorry you had the date from hell, I most definitely plan on having a little chat with him as soon as I get a chance."

"Gail don't worry about it, I'm over it. I cursed him out and cried so it's all good, really you don't have to check him.

"Oh no, you better believe I'm going to rip him a new butthole when I talk to him. I don't play about my friends, you didn't deserve that and he's going to get an earful." Says Gail!

Gail's attention abruptly moved to her wailing cellphone.

"Shoot girl, my alarm just reminded me that I have a hair appointment with Morgan in an hour, come ride with me?"

Morgan's salon was packed as usual. The ladies checked in with Morgan's assistant Nikki and sat in the waiting area.

"I hope her date with Raven was more successful than mine was," says Zaya.

"From the voicemail she left me I highly doubt it," says Gail.

"Hey ladies!" Morgan greeted both Gail and Zaya with hugs.

"Come on back with me and I'll have Monique wash your hair while I set up for you,

Zaya bring your ass too so you can participate in the gossip" said Morgan.

Gail sat at the bowl and leaned back, "Don't think because I'm under this water I won't be able to hear you because I will. Now what happened with you and Raven?" ask Gail.

"To be honest Gail I'm quite embarrassed by the whole situation," says Morgan.

"Girl we've all had dates from hell, you know no one is going to judge you." Gail says.

Morgan sits down in her styling chair and twirls around a few times inhaling and exhaling.

"Would you just tell us and stop with all of the drama!" says Zaya.

Morgan stops spinning and looks at Zaya, "He said a similar statement to me that night."

"Okay well we would like to know what happened so spit it out Chile." Gail says.

"The first half of our date was amazing, he got in the limo looking and smelling good. He was such a gentleman, he opened doors for me and pulled out my chair. Conversation over dinner was light but very stimulating, I learned a few things about him and him about me. He complimented me all night and made me giggle like a school girl, but unfortunately he seen right through me. I went to the bathroom to brag to Nikki about how I thought I had him right where I wanted him, I was going to work my way into his pockets. Well when I was about to return to our table one of the waitresses told me that he had left, which was later confirmed by the waiter that worked our table. I ran out of the hotel and caught him in the nick of time before he left. I confronted him like he had done me dirty, I told him that he couldn't treat me like he does all of the other women in his life. I was not some whore, and he said that in all actuality I was a whore. He said that he knew what type of woman I was all along, he knew what my agenda was from jump. The last thing he said was he suggest I tighten up my game before I hunt down my next victim; that was it, he left."

The salon was completely silent; it was Gail that broke the silence.

"And how did his words make you feel Morgan?"

"It made me feel like I was just hit by a bus, I guess the truth always hurts."

"Now Morgan you are not a slut, don't even think that about yourself." said Nikki.

"Nikki please okay, until that moment I thought I had buried my feelings with Quentin. When he died I emotionally shut down, I vowed not to ever love another man because I didn't want another him. I promised myself that no man would ever get close to me again. I made it up in my mind that all a man could offer me was fine dining, paid bills and shopping sprees; hell I didn't even buy this shop with my own money. This shop was built on the dollars of a lawyer, a celebrity chef and the owner of a fortune five hundred company. I slept with them all to get my business, my car and a lot of other irrelevant things like clothes and jewelry. Raven was telling the truth, I'm no better than he is, in fact I may be worse." Taken over by emotion, Morgan ran into the bathroom sobbing.

Zaya looks over at Gail, "Well, looks like you have two assholes to scold now."

Gail was furious with Raven and Nathaniel's behavior on their dates with the ladies. She was going to get to the bottom of why Nathaniel purposely sabotaged him and Zaya's date and why Raven decided to take truth serum before his date with Morgan. She calls Nathaniel first but his phone went straight to voicemail. "That's okay I'll see you at the hospital after I'm done with the other knucklehead." She calls Raven and wakes him out of his sleep.

"Raven wake up we need to talk, you need to call Morgan and apolo..."

"I know Gail, I've already decided on that."

"Wait a minute, have I dialed the correct number? This is Raven Rahkel Robinson the tennis champion right?"

"Shut the hell up Gail, I've thought long and hard about this, you know I have issues."

"Yes I know I just can't believe that you're actually not blaming anyone for your behavior, you're finally taking responsibility for your own actions. I'm proud of your Rave."

"But you know I told her the truth... don't you?"

"Yea I know that you told her the truth and she knows it too, that's why it hurt her so bad. Truth can be more devastating than a lie unfortunately. Well at least y'all know that y'all have one thing in common," says Gail.

"And what the hell is that Gail?" ask Raven.

"Both of y'all are generous with your genitals, get some rest Rave."

Gail hung up on Raven in the midst of a profanity filled rant.

"One idiot down and one more to go."

She knew that it was going to be a battle with Nathaniel, he is so stubborn, so set in his ways. She asked the nurse at the front desk where he was and she pointed towards the waiting room. There he was holding a little girl in his arms just as happy as he could be. She looks about three or four years old and she is clearly smitten by him. He was so into the little girl that he hadn't noticed that Gail had come into the waiting area.

"Look you were right Dr. Thompson, the lump behind my belly button is gone!"

"I told you Olivia it would disappear like magic, I'm so glad that you came back to see me." He begins to tickle her causing her to release high pitched giggles.

"Okay Olivia it's time to go, give Dr. Thompson a nice big hug and tell him good-bye." Mr. Korver says.

She hugs him for dear life and planted a big kiss on his cheek.

"Take care Olivia! Come back and visit me sometimes." He yells.

"Are children the only human beings that get to experience the softer side of you?"

"Gail what are you doing here? Well I already know why you're here, and you've wasted your time." Says Nathaniel.

"How so Nathaniel? I just want to know why you deliberately ruined your date with my good friend Zaya, she's a good woman you know."

"I'm a grown man I don't have to explain myself. I agreed to go on your date and I did. It was nowhere in the rules stating that I had to like it."

"That's your problem Nathaniel, you hurt people and leave them clueless as to why. You are like a thief in the night, you take and leave the person who you've taken from wondering who in the hell stole from them and why. Now let's be real, how fair is that?" says Gail.

"You think I don't know she's a good woman? You think I don't know how beautiful she is? It surprised me that she took all of that insult for as long as she did, but she did it out of love for you. She was actually willing to look past all of that and try to get to know me. She made me uncomfortable with her patience and poise. When she stepped into that elevator with tears falling from her eyes it did something to me, I actually feel bad about tearing her down like that. It's over and done now, I can't change the past." says Nathaniel.

"No you can't, but you can offer an apology to wrong and right and go from there. She was hurt deeply by your cruelty but she doesn't hate you, believe me I've known the girl for years, she would've tried to hurt you by now. So why don't you give her a call and invite her out for a cup of coffee to clear the air." say Gail.

"Okay I'll do that."

"Good, I must go now. Go back in there and fix some babies."

"Hey Gail..."

She turns and looks slightly over her right shoulder.

"Thanks, I appreciate everything you've done for me."

She nods and continues walking to her car.

"And they say there's no such thing as miracles."

"Those who cannot change their minds cannot change anything."~ George Bernard Shaw

~Nathaniel~

Nathaniel left the hospital feeling nervous about talking to Zaya again. He's never apologized to anyone for anything ever in his life. He's always believed that 'I'm sorry' held no meaning or value. Rachel use to say it in the beginning, when the abuse first started but after a few times I think she realized that we both knew that she wasn't sorry for any of the things that she did to me so she stopped saying it. A call from his father snatches him back from going down memory lane.

"Hey dad what's up?"

"You should come see her son, she's not looking too good."

"Okay dad if it will get you off of my back, I'll go and see her, satisfied?"

"You just don't know how happy you've made me son, you're doing the right thing."

Nathaniel spent a few more minutes on the phone with his father before hanging up to call Zaya. He'd dial six numbers but just couldn't bring himself to press the last digit. He finally decided to put it off until he got home and got some liquor in his system. If he's going to apologize to her and mean it, he's going to need some liquor courage to help him out.

He walks into his home and immediately goes upstairs into his bedroom to raid the mini bar. His choice of drink for this task is Conjure Cognac. He takes a couple of swigs and stares at his cell phone.

"Fuck it, let's get this over with." He drains the remainder of his drink and dials her number. He was just about to hang up on the third ring but she answered.

"Hello"

"Hello Zaya its Nathaniel."

"I know how may I help you sir?"

"Well I was calling to... um, I'm calling to... to um..."

"Nathaniel spit it out Jesus Christ."

"I'm sorry for hurting your feelings. I'm sorry for being an asshole from the very first day that we met. I'm sorry for treating you like less than a person and I was hoping... well I was hoping that you'll forgive me, will you?"

Zaya laughs, "You sound like you're asking me to marry you, and to answer your question yes I'll forgive you as long as you promise to work on that. I may forgive you but you might not be so lucky with the next woman."

"Thank you Zaya."

"You're welcome Meany Pie."

"Meany Pie?"

"Yep, you're a cutie pie but mean as hell."

He laughs out loud and says, "Well if I'm Meany Pie you can just be cutie pie, how about that?"

"Dr. Nathaniel Thompson you have yourself a deal."

Nathaniel and Zaya talked and laughed like old friends from high school that day, they didn't hang up with each other until four hours later.

The following day Nathaniel decides to go see his mother in the nursing home. After pacing for about an hour he finally worked up the nerves to drive to the facility. He finds a park on a side street next to the building. He sits there with one foot out of the car and the other one still inside. He pulls his foot back in and shuts the door. He grabs his phone and calls the last person he's talked to.

"Hey Zaya, can you meet me somewhere?"

"Things don't happen for a reason, we make reasons out of things that happen."~ Michael P. Naughton

~Morgan~

On Wednesday's the salon closes up shop around three p.m. Morgan usually stays behind to clean and organize paperwork while her staff heads home early. There wasn't much to clean this particular day but a couple of towels to be thrown in the laundry and a few garbage cans to be emptied. She gathers all of the garbage bags and drags them through the back door into the alley, she sees Tim her business neighbor and sparks up a conversation.

"Hey Tim you're taking a break?"

"Yea I'm puffing on this cig for a minute before I go back in there, what's up with you?"

"Oh I'm just doing a little cleaning before I leave for the day, you know I close early on Wednesdays."

"Yea I know but why? You're missing out on some good money aren't you?"

"I have my reasons. Well I'll talk to you later Tim." Morgan opens the back door and walks in. She doesn't hear the door slam so she turns around to see why, Tim caught it and came inside.

"What's up Tim you need something?" ask Morgan.

"Yea you," he says.

"Boy stop playing, you've been looking in my face for a while now and haven't said one word, so why now?"

He starts to walk towards her and before he even makes it close to her, the smell of liquor attacks her nostrils. He stands in front of her and her stomach instantly begins to flip.

"Damn Tim you've been hitting the bottle heavy today haven't you? Damns" she attempts to step back but he pulls her close to him.

"Baby we turn up every day all day, so you're telling me that you never looked at me like that before? You've never wanted to see what I'm working with?" he asks.

"Um no I haven't, so would you let me go thanks." Again she attempts to move away but he holds her tighter, it suddenly hit her that she may be in danger.

He leans forward and aggressively begins to kiss her, moving his liquored flavored tongue around the inside of her mouth, coating her face with his saliva. She finds the strength to eventually break away from him and run. She wasn't fast enough because he caught her by the hair, captured her throat and threw her against one of the mirrors in another stylist station. The force of the impact shatters the mirror cutting her back up, she's swinging and kicking but it's making no difference. He lifts her again, off of her feet by her throat and slams her down to the floor with so much force that it knocks the wind out of her. She lies helplessly on the salon floor crying as he mounts her and rips her top in half.

"You parade around here like you're too good for me, denying me of what I want. Once I give you this dick, you're going to be asking for it daily." He smiles as he begins to unbuckle his jeans.

After talking to Gail, Raven knew that his decision to set things straight with Morgan was the right thing to do. He remembered the name of her salon from their dinner conversation so he googled the salon's address, and saw that it was a quick fifteen-minute drive from where he was. He finds a parking space right in front of the salon which if anybody who has ever been on the north side of Chicago knows that finding a park in these parts was practically impossible. He grabs the roses he picked up along the way from out of the back seat of his truck and smiled.

"Damn I must really like her because I bought her roses, drove myself and came to see her without my bodyguards, yea she better accept my apology or it's a done deal." He walks up to the entrance and tries to pull open the door but it's locked. He looks through the glass of the door and sees a lady lying on the floor but he can't tell if it's Morgan or not. He presses his face against the window and uses his hands to block the sun out to see better inside. He sees a man appear from around a corner while stroking his jank. He says something to the woman on the floor and then kicks her. Raven instincts kicked in and he found a sizeable stone in front of a neighboring shop to break the glass to unlock the door. The man was so focused on the woman on the floor that he didn't hear the shattering glass. Once he got close enough without being detected he could then see that the woman on the floor was in deed Morgan, he lost it. He rushes the guy and punches him in the temple, knocking him off of Morgan. Raven begins to kick and stomp Tim until blood splatters on his sneakers.

"RAVEN STOP! Please!" screams Morgan.

Raven has stomped Tim unconscious. He scoops Morgan up from the floor and grimaces when she moans in pain. He carries her out of the salon to his truck, and lays her in the back seat.

"Raven we have to call the police," she whispers.

"I will just stay here, I'll be right back."

Raven picks up the stone he used to break the glass and dials nine-one-one as he entered back into the salon.

"Hello I would like to report a rape at the 'In Hair' salon on 1121 N. Touhy Ave. The victim's name is Morgan and she's the owner of the salon. I came to see her and found a man assaulting her. I knocked him out and carried her to my car, she's in bad shape she's needs an ambulance. My name is Raven Robinson, yes that Raven Robinson. Really you wanna do this right now? Broad send an ambulance and the police right now." Raven hung up with the groupie dispatcher to find the dude he beat down awakening. Raven pushed Tim over onto his back so he could look him in the eyes.

"So you like to rape women huh? You like to steal women's goodies and shit? Well if you haven't learned anything in your entire life, you've learned something today; it's one thing that I can't stand, and that's a thief." Raven takes the stone and throws it down onto Tim's penis causing him to scream out in agony.

"The police are on their way you disgusting piece of shit." Raven walks out to see the ambulance and police driving up.

"Over here, she's in the back seat of my truck" yells Raven.

The paramedics removes Morgan from the truck, places her onto a gurney and then into the ambulance. The police escorts Tim out in handcuffs and questions Raven about the incident. He uses his celebrity charm to get the chance to ride with Morgan in the ambulance instead of going straight to the police station to answer questions. He convinces them to follow the ambulance to the emergency room to continue the questioning there.

Whatever the doctors gave Morgan for the pain knocked her right out, she slept a little over two hours.

Morgan awakes groggy and holding a male's hand, she looks up to her right to see Raven staring at her.

"Hi," she mumbles.

"Hi beautiful, how do you feel?"

"I'm aching but I've felt worse before, how are you?"

"My temper finally settled I'm calmer now, listen I thought about calling Gail, but I thought it would be best if you did, given the sensitivity of the situation." says Raven.

A nurse came into the room to perform a rape kit but Morgan explained that Tim never got the chance to penetrate her, Raven stopped him.

She squeezes his hand and looks at him, "He saved my life."

"Forgiveness is the needle that knows how to mend."~ Jewel

~Gail~

Gail arrives at her parents' home short-tempered and cranky, her illness is getting the best of her today. There are days were she feels normal, like there's nothing wrong at all but then there are days like this that reminds her of her reality. Today is Monroe's birthday and her parents invited family and friends over to a last minute birthday party for him. She really didn't want to come but her mom insisted that she see as much family as she can now. She takes a deep breath and rings the doorbell.

"Hey honey, I'm glad that you came."

"Hey mom."

"Gail you don't look so good baby, let's go sit down, I'll fix you a plate." Her mother escorts her into the living room. It was like her family had seen a ghost, because they stared at her like she was something they've never seen before. She over hears one of her cousins whisper, "Is that Gail?" she knows that she looks different, she's lost so much weight and her eyes look weary. Her mother also sensed the awkwardness and intervened.

"Look everybody, Gail's here," says Mrs. Shannon.

"Hey everyone, long time no see," Gail says.

Gail's little cousin Justin walks up to her and waves his finger for her to get down to his level.

"Gail is it true that you're going to heaven soon?"

"Justin! Get back over here and stop asking people about their business!" his mother says.

"Well mommy you ask me about my business all of the time, you always ask me am I finished when I'm on the potty." He leans closer to Gail and whispers, "Mommy hasn't learned about privacy and personal space yet."

"Boy you are three and a half, you don't have any business now get over here."

"Hold on Leah let me answer his question." She scoops him into her arms and kisses his forehead, "Yes Justin, soon I'll be in heaven."

"Well I don't want you to go yet, can't you tell God no thank you you've changed your mind?"

"No, I'm sorry I can't." She hugs him tight and gave him a raspberry, "I'm going to miss you Justin."

"I'm going to miss you too Gail, okay I have to go play now." He kisses her on the cheek and runs off.

Every face in the family room is sad, but Gail manages to keep her composure.

"Hey now, I'm still here; it's Monroe's birthday, let's have some fun."

It takes a while for everyone to shake the sadness off and enjoy the party but eventually they did. Everyone was here except for the birthday boy which wasn't surprising to Gail at all. Monroe hasn't ever cared about anyone but himself so it wouldn't surprise her if he didn't show up at all.

The music is blasting, the children are running around the backyard having fun. The men are helping her dad with the grilling and a few of the ladies are in the kitchen with her and her mom. All of the meat and side dishes are finally done and everyone is ready to eat. Gail helps her mom serve the children first and then the adults. Gail takes her mother's hand and starts to dance when she hears her song by Syleena Johnson and Musiq Soulchild come through the speakers.

"I need you to feel this fire... cause I'm burning up, burning for your love... I need you to feel this fire..." Gail sings as she twirls her mother.

"Aye this is my song!"

Gail and Mrs. Shannon stops dancing to look at Monroe, he's sloppy drunk and when he drinks all hell usually breaks loose.

"Monroe, how are you going to show up to your own party late and drunk?" ask Mrs. Shannon.

"Like I just did mother. Hey sis you look bad, I mean really bad, what's wrong with you? Oh yea I forgot your about to croak any minute now, where's dad?"

Mrs. Shannon and Gail simultaneously look at each other and begin fixing plates again. After everyone had their plates Gail and Mrs. Shannon join the family in the dining room.

"We're eating inside everyone, it's too many gnats flying around out there." Says Mr. Shannon.

Monroe is so drunk that he's tripping over his own feet spilling beer all over the carpet.

"Monroe! Look at what you're doing! I can't believe you came here like this; I'm so disappointed in you." Yells Mrs. Shannon.

"It's not the first time I've disappointed you mother. Calm down it's my birthday, I can do whatever I want, just focus on Gail like you always do, don't worry about me." Says Monroe.

"Monroe can you for once act like you have an ounce of sense, mom and dad threw this party for you when they didn't have to and you being disrespectful. You are not a child anymore Monroe you are a grown ass man so the things that were acceptable then are not acceptable now." Says Gail.

"Look Gail I'm not in the mood to argue with you, I don't feel good."

"You don't feel good? I DON'T FEEL GOOD MONROE! I hurt! I ache! I be in pain so unbearable that I want to take my own life. Not only did I find out that my husband was sleeping with my brother, I had to plan his got damn funeral, but do you see me walking around acting a damn fool?! NO MONROE YOU DON'T!" screams Gail.

Leah senses that it is about to get real ugly so she rounds up all of the children and leads them outside into the yard to play.

"What, wait a minute; Monroe you slept with your sister's husband?" ask Mr. Shannon.

"Monroe, how could you do that to Gail?" questioned Mrs. Shannon.

"Oh please he wasn't the first man Gail and I shared, she knows that." says Monroe.

Monroe takes a dinner roll from his father's plate and sprawls out on the couch.

"Matter of fact you should thank me Gail for revealing to you who you were in relationships with. You tried to pretend like you didn't know that your high school love Terrence and I were knocking boots, the man use to get a hard on every time he saw me for God sakes, oh and you should thank me too dad."

"Excuse me, thank you for what?"

"The Brent Mason case you were in trouble; the defense was eating you alive. You were going to lose; Judge Sloan still calls me for late night rendezvous to this very day." says Monroe.

"Monroe that's enough you have gone too far!" yells Mrs. Shannon.

"Yea yea yea I'm going to sleep, wake me up in the morning when you make breakfast, okay mom." Monroe blows Gail a kiss.

"You say I look bad Monroe but you do to, sick?" ask Gail.

"Since you're so damn nosy, yes I am I can't seem to shake this flu. But I'm Monroe Giovanni Shannon, there's nothing that can hold me down." He replies.

"The flu doesn't last this long little brother; you should've stuck around at the hospital that night."

"And why should I have done that? The wife not the mistress has the upper hand." Monroe says.

Monroe rolls his eyes and tries to walk past Gail but she stops him by placing her hand on his chest.

"Because you would've discovered that my husband and your lover was H.I.V positive."

The color immediately drained from Monroe's face, he hugs himself and sits down in the love seat.

"I forgive you brother, I've accepted my fate and now it's time to accept yours." She walks over to her parents' hug and kisses them each good night, stopping at the family room entrance she looks over her shoulder.

"Happy Birthday Monroe."

An apology is the super glue of life; it can repair just about anything."~ Lynn Johnston

~Nathaniel & Zaya~

For the past hour Zaya has tried to convince Nathaniel to go inside the nursing home to see his mother, he refuses to even take his seatbelt off.

"If you don't get this out of your system now it's going to continue to eat at you for the rest of your life. You have an opportunity to free yourself of those childhood demons, a lot of people don't get that chance Nathaniel."

He leans over and kisses her, "Thank you; let's go, I'm ready to get this over with."

Nathaniel and Zaya walks in on Nathaniel's father singing to his mother.

"Son, you kept your word. I thought you had changed your mind." says Mr. Thompson.

"I almost did, Dad this is my friend Zaya Martin, Zaya this is my father Nicholas Thompson, and that's Rachel."

"Look Rachel our son is here to see you."

She slowly turns to look at Nathaniel. She
looks him up and down before resting her eyes
on his.

"What's your name?" she asked.

"Nathaniel"

"You look at me with hate in your eyes,
was I a bad mother?"

"You were the worst mother a child
could have," Nathaniel says.

"NATHANIEL!" yells Mr. Thompson.

"Well she asked and I answered dad,
okay I think I'm about done here, good-bye."

"What did I do? Why was I a bad
mother?" inquired Rachel.

Nathaniel turns his back to her and raises his
shirt.

"When I was six years old you got mad at
me for calling you mama and not Rachel so
you took a pocket knife and carved your initial
right here." He ran his fingers along the scar
and continued, "And then when I was seven I
accidentally broke your glass giraffe, it
shattered into twenty pieces. You made me get
into the shower and wait for you, so I did as I

was told. You whacked me with a thick leather belt twenty times drawing blood from me."

"Oh my god Nathaniel," whispers Zaya.

"I can go on if you like Rachel, I can continue to tell you how you're the reason why I hated women and didn't respect them. My childhood was a nightmare, I was afraid to breathe around you, I feared for my life every single day because I didn't know when I was going to do something to set you off." He sat next to her on her bed, "Do you remember when you would cook just for you to eat and I would go days without eating until you decided to feed me? You kept a damn chain and lock on the refrigerator."

Rachel covers her face and begins to weep.

"Oh no Rachel that's not it, I have more."

"Son that's enough, she gets the point."

"No one ever said it was enough when she would lock me in my room twenty-four hours at a time when she brought men home, and then she'd beat me because I would urinate on myself because I couldn't get out of the room to use the bathroom. No one ever said it was enough when she would use the bottoms of my feet to put out her cigarettes.

No one ever said it was enough when I was crying begging her to stop and she just smiled and enjoyed the pain she was inflicting onto me. Where were you dad to say Rachel that's enough?"

Rachel reaches for Nathaniel and hugs him.

"I'm sorry, I'm so sorry, please forgive me. I don't know why I did those things, I wish I'd hadn't done them, I'm so sorry."

He removes her arms from around his shoulders and walks to the door.

"Yea I wish you didn't either."

Nathaniel walks Zaya to her car and thanks her again for coming through.

"I really appreciate you for doing this Zaya."

"No problem, anytime."

"I would like to make up for our last date, maybe we could try it again?"

"I'd like that, how about a picnic on the lake?" says Zaya.

"Cool, how about tomorrow around three thirty?" asked Nathaniel.

"Perfect, so I'll bring the goodies and you bring the wine and blankets."

"Sounds good, I'll see you then." He meets her half way for a kiss, she attempts to come down from her tip toes but he cuffed her butt and held her in place.

"Bye Nathaniel."

"Bye Zaya." He opens her car door and watches her drive off.

"Damn those lips are going to get me in trouble."

Witnessing Nathaniel vent to his mother about his upbringing made her want to confront Kenneth. He crushed her heart with the stunt he pulled on the eve of their wedding day. It was time for her to let go of the baggage and move on. She'd seen a softer more vulnerable side of Nathaniel tonight and she liked it. The way he confided in her... the way he looked into her eyes and kissed her was so sexy, and according to her damped underwear, her vagina thought so too.

She was freshly showered when she climbed into bed with a glass of wine. She went to send Nathaniel a good night text when she notices she has a voicemail from Gail.

"Zaya, Morgan called me, she was leaving the hospital from an attempted rape today at her shop, but by the grace of God Raven was there to prevent it. It was on CBS news; I'll call you as soon as I get more information."

Zaya grabbed her laptop and went to the CBS news Chicago website to check for Morgan's incident, under local news it read:

Celebrity Tennis player Raven Robinson saves woman from attacker.

Zaya gasp as she read the report, she makes a mental note to call Morgan tomorrow to check on her. She thanks God for Raven being there to intervene, she thanks God for Nathaniel finally opening up about his past, she prays for everyone that she knows and for everyone she doesn't.

"There is never a time or place for true love. It happens accidentally in a heartbeat, in a single flashing throbbing moment."~ Sarah Dessen

~Morgan & Raven~

Raven walks Morgan to her front door and hugs her.

"Give me a call if you need anything alright? I'll catch you later."

"Wait Raven, I don't want to be alone tonight, please stay." She pulls his face to hers and kisses him.

"Morgan, are you sure about this? You're pretty bruised and he almost..."

"Shhhh, I'm sure; I know what I want." she says.

He follows her into the house and into the bedroom, she instantly starts to undress him.

She whispers against his skin, "Take a shower with me."

They explore one another under the steamy water as they wash away the day's drama. He carries her to the bed and places her down gently.

"Are you sure that you want to do this? I don't want to hurt you any further," he asks.

"Please Raven, let me feel you."

He wants her just as much as she wants him and he was about to prove it. He lifts himself over her and drags his fingers gently from her face down to her ankle. He slowly raises her left leg burying his head into her inner thigh, kissing and sucking, licking and biting her creamy skin. He slides his hands under her backside lifting her to his face as he began to plant kisses on her moistness. His tongue moves horizontally on her vertical walls. He is all over the place. She shivers as he trails his tongue from her neck down her stomach, moaning when he parts her womanhood with his fingers, he stops, resting his lips upon hers.

"You are soaking wet, you want it? Ask me for it." He spanks her juice box until she cries out to him.

"Raven, baby please; I need it, I want it, please give it to me."

He leans back on his knees and strokes his penis. He can see the yearning in her eyes and he knew that she could see the hunger in his.

He uses his tool to slap her inner thighs and vagina, making her gasp.

"Eeny, Meeny, Miny, Moe... should I give this pussy my mighty pole..." He lifts himself over her and enters her slowly, with every thrust he'd bite her bottom lip and he didn't stop until every inch of him was inside of her. She arches her back and wraps her legs around his waist crossing her feet on his backside.

"You feel so damn good, do it just like that, don't stop." She spoke into his mouth as he grunts at the tightness and warmth of her. He lifts her up and squeezes her cheeks as he bites her neck and quickens the pace. He has her singing like a bird, she gyrates her hips to his rhythm while trying to contain the moans escaping from her mouth. She uses her hips to help guide him on his back, she is now on top clamping down on his penis like a vice grip, riding him like a jock in a horse race.

"Yea baby squeeze this dick, shit Morgan!"

He threw his head back grunting, biting his lip. He's let her have enough control, now it was time for him to bring it on home. He flips her onto her back and pulls out.

"Turn that ass over, I wanna see it jiggle while I'm hitting it."

She arches her back when he grips her hair and yanks her head back. His thrust became deeper... harder... stronger; her muscles are tightening around his tool and she can feel her release nearing. He bends down and whispers in her ear.

"Are you going to cum for me?"

"Yeesssss Rave... oh yeessss... I'm gonna... Oh God!" She screams and shudders, snatching the sheet off of the bed. He pounds her feverishly before crying out her name and collapsing on top of her.

He rolls to his side never letting go of her, kissing the back of her neck he pulls her into his chest, she turns to face him.

"That was amazing, I really needed that."

"That was amazing and we most definitely should do this again," he says.

She kisses him on the chin, "I agree." She hears him say something along the lines of 'seconds' but she was exhausted from the day and the closeness of him relaxed her that she drifted off to sleep in his arms.

He tries to ignore his ringtone but whoever is calling him really wants to talk to him. He gently pulls his arm from under Morgan and snatches his pants from the floor, it's his coach.

"Hello?"

"Rave, turn to channel five and watch the news, you have to see this."

Raven retrieves Morgan's television remotes from the nightstand on her side of the bed, he turns to channel five and sees a picture of Dale.

"From studio five, this is NBC five news today at six. Dale Trent made headlines for being attacked by fellow pro tennis player Raven Robinson a few weeks ago, this time he's in the news for domestic violence. Good morning everyone and thank you for being with us on this Thursday September fifth, I'm Carrie Strong."

"And I'm Emmanuel Stint. The police were called to the Trent residence around nine fifteen p.m. by some neighbors who said they heard a woman screaming please stop, I'm sorry. The police arrived to find Trinity

Trent, Dale Trent's wife with a bloody face; it is reported that Dale attacked his wife when he found naked pictures that she'd text to his tennis coach Carl Struthers. There are no further developments on this story."

"Should've known better Dale; if she cheated on me, she'll cheat on you. Whores are creatures of habit." His phone vibrates in his hand startling him.

"Hey Rave its Jazz, I'm texting you to tell you that I'm leaving the house today for good. I've thought long and hard about this and I've come to the conclusion that I do in fact love you and I can't pretend to not be fazed by you being with other women. It's not that you're a bad guy but I deserve more; I need more. Well it's been real, I'll definitely miss you, but I think this is the best thing to do for me; Good-bye Mr. Robinson, smooches."

He sent her a kiss back and wished her well. He was actually proud of her; he always thought that she was smarter than how she portrayed herself. He looks over at Morgan and studies her face as she sleeps. She was so beautiful; he smiles at the images of the love faces she made while they were making love. He ran his fingers along a bruise on her arm; he knows she will be sore when she wakes up, so he went to start a warm bath for her and breakfast.

"I accept reality and dare not question it."~ Walt Whitman

~Gail~

She tries to hold herself together as she looks at burial plots. I know people think that she is crazy for planning her own funeral but she's never been the type to put her responsibilities off on other people. She'd done a good job of not crying but once she seen the looks on both her mother and Zaya's faces, she broke down into tears. She asked them to come with her to choose a grave, headstone and casket. It all became too much for her mother and she ran out of the cemetery.

"I'm so sorry Gail I can't do this!"

Zaya turned to Gail with tears in her eyes, "I'm trying Gail, I'm really trying but this is so hard to do."

"I know honey, I know."

Zaya stuck it out with Gail for the entire day and helped organize everything for her departure; all there was left to do was the writing of the will. She said her good-byes to Zaya and headed home, she was in desperate need of a nap. This whole thing on top of all the emotions has worn her out. She entered her home to find her mother sitting in her living room.

"Mom what are you doing here? I thought you went home when you left the cemetery." said Gail.

"No, I didn't, I drove around for a bit... Gail sit down, I want to talk to you about something."

"Wait mom, do I need a bottle of wine?"

"Yea, grab two, one for you and one for me."

Gail came back with two bottles of wine and glasses.

"Here you go Mom, what's up?"

"Thank you. Gail I've had a lot of regrets since me and your father found out about your health. I painfully realized that I wasn't the most nurturing mother that I should've been. I raised you with tough love and Monroe with nothing but love and look how you both turned out. I have one child that any parent would love to call their own while my other child act like he was raised by a pack of wolves. I'm here to tell you that if I ever made you feel not good enough, if I ever made you feel like you had to work for my love, if I ever made you feel obligated to make me happy before yourself; I would like to say I'm sorry. I can't let you leave without knowing that regardless of everything that's happened, you'll always be my baby."

"Mom you don't know how relieved I am to hear you say this, because you have made me feel all of those ways. My entire life I've spent it doing what you've wanted me to do or what you thought I should do. The only thing I did for me was marry Chaz, and that's the one time I wish I would've listened to you."

"How have you been dealing with his death?" asked her mother.

"I've been okay; I do miss him though. Even though he was a lying no good cheating bastard, I miss him. I guess I get it from daddy. No matter what, I always try and find the good in people and hold onto that. Mom you may have been a little harsh with your tactics but you raised a mighty strong woman." says Gail.

"Cheers to that."

Gail and her mother talked like old girlfriends for the first time in their life. They opened up to each other about love, life, friends and family. She really felt a genuine connection between them.

Tossing the fourth piece of paper into a garbage pail, Gail starts over from the top writing out her last will and testament.

I, Gail Miranda Washington of....

"God I can't do this!" she begins to violently cry; her whole body was shaking. She wipes her face when she sees Morgan's photo appear on her cellphone.

"Hel... hello?"

"Hey Gail how are you?" ask Morgan.

"Oh Girl I'm a huge mess, what about you?"

"I feel much better, I'm sorry I'm just getting back with you. Yesterday was interesting."

"Interesting, what was interesting about it? I would think that yesterday was crazy and or scary but not interesting." says Gail.

"It was crazy and scary at the beginning but it was interesting later on."

"Morgan I need you to explain that to me because I'm not getting it."

"Raven and I made love last night and it was out of this world. I never came so hard in my entire sexual career."

Gail jumps up with a big kool-aid smile on her face.

"Morgan are you serious?! I need details!"

Morgan told Gail how Raven saved her and stayed with her at the hospital and how he was so protective and loving.

"Wait a minute are we talking about the same Raven Robinson because I'm having a hard time believing that he made you a bubble bath, cooked you breakfast and gave you a massage. Damn Morgan your coochie must be platinum!" Gail says jokingly.

"Girl not at all, he did all of that because he wanted to. From our conversation this morning I think we're exclusively dating now. I told him he had to kick out all of those scallywags living in his house, those broads have to go!"

"I know that's right girl, let it be known that the champ is off the market."

"Girl I'm sorry but I need to turn it in right now, I'm exhausted. Today was super emotional." says Gail.

"Okay girl thanks again for checking up on my well-being." says Morgan.

"No problem sweetie, that's what I do; I care about people."

> *"Sometimes the heart sees what is invisible to the eye."~ Jackson Brown Jr.*

~Zaya & Nathaniel~

It is about three o'clock when Zaya arrives at Northwestern Hospital to meet up with Nathaniel for their picnic on the beach. Not only did the basket of goodies look good but so did she. She was wearing a denim short romper that accentuated her curves. She crinkled her hair pulling the top half back into a ponytail allowing the bottom half to hang along her shoulders. It's been a long time since she's put thought into looking nice for a man, for some reason she wanted to impress him.

When she walks into the hospital she sees him in the waiting area talking to a half-naked female. She is light skinned with a long fiery red nappy weave. She has on booty shorts that display all of her dimples and stretch marks. Ole girl has a tattoo on her right shoulder that looks familiar. As she wrecks her brain trying to think of where she knows this girl from she sees him, he walks up behind her and wraps his arm around her waist.

"Kenneth..." she mumbles.

Zaya can't help but walk towards them, she had to see him up close and personal once more. She was so focused on the side of Kenneth's face that she didn't see Jake in her path knocking a cup of coffee out of his hand.

"Oh I'm so sorry, excuse... Jake?"

He looks up from wiping coffee off of his shoes and smiles.

"Zaya? Hey girl what's up? You're not coming to set anyone on fire are you?" he said jokingly.

"No I'm here to meet someone for lunch, you must be here with Kenneth and ole girl."

"Yea their son Kari was on an escalator with his ding bat of a mother when she let his hand go to send a text causing him to lose his balance. His hand got caught in the escalator severing a few of his fingers, they managed to save all but one, poor baby lost a lot of blood." says Jake.

Together they walk over and join the couple and Nathaniel.

"Because of how much blood Kari lost we asked you, Crystal and Jake to volunteer blood to see if we could find a matching blood type for him. Now it's not uncommon for children to have a different blood type from their parents. We each have two genes for the A, B and O blood types; A and B are dominant, so if a person has an A or a B as well as an O, their blood type will be A or B. But they can pass on to O. Two parents who are A or B but each have the O gene can have a child who is type O. This is because both parents passed on the recessive O gene. On the other hand, if both parents are type O, it means neither have an A or B gene, so they cannot pass on anything but the O gene. The child can only be type O. If one parent is type A and the other is type B it is also possible for a child to get both of these and be type AB." explains Nathaniel.

"Dr. Thompson speak English, what are you trying to say." ask Kenneth.

Nathaniel took a deep breath, "Both of you are in the AB blood group, but Kari's has type O blood; neither one of you possess the O gene; I'm sorry Mr. Glover but it's impossible for you to be Kari's father."

Just like the first, the cup of coffee Jake was clutching slipped right from his hands splashing on everyone in the vicinity. A flash of fear appeared in Crystal eyes, she slowly began to back away from Kenneth. Jake drops his head when his best friend looks back at him.

"Go on Doctor Thompson, you have more to add on to that statement." says Kenneth.

"Unfortunately I do. Like I said we asked all three of you to donate blood and um..."

"And my best buddy back there, blood matches Kari's, is that what you were about to say?"

"Yes," Says Nathaniel.

"Baby I'm sorry, it was only one time I swear. I love you..."

"I'm giving you exactly one hour to pack all of you and Kari's shit and get out of my house. If you are still there when I come home, I'm going to jail for murder. Do I make myself clear?"

Crystal runs past Kenneth sobbing and jiggling all over the place looking like the Kool-aid pitcher bursting through the wall so Zaya sticks her foot out and trips her, causing her to flip over the hospital janitor's cart.

"THAT'S FOR FUCKING MY FIANCE" shouts Zaya.

Kenneth turns to Jake and scowls.

"My best friend, my buddy, my homey, my brother; let me holler at you outside real quick."

"Come on Ken man I'm not on that, I'm not trying to fight..." Jake's jaw cracked from the force of Kenneth's right hook, he hit the floor dizzy.

"You can take this ass whipping now or take it later, it's up to you."

"Kenneth no!" Zaya grabs him and drags him outside. She guides him a safe distance into the parking lot to give Jake a chance to leave without getting hurt.

"Kenneth what is beating him up going to solve?"

"What was setting me on fire going to solve?" he retorted.

"I was mad hell! You broke my heart!" replies Zaya.

"And I'm mad as hell! They broke my heart! I love that little boy! And wait a minute you just mad tripped the shit out of Crystal as payback for sleeping with me!"

"Never mind that, that was for laughs. Kenneth you can still love him, what's wrong with him having two fathers? You two have a chance to make him feel like the luckiest boy in the world." says Zaya.

"I guess this is karma huh? I hurt you so bad and I never got the chance to apologize for my actions. Believe it or not Zaya I really did love you but I was only marrying you because you wanted to get married. I wasn't ready and I was too much of a coward to tell you. I hope you have found it somewhere in that big heart of yours to forgive me." he says.

She points to her heart, "You destroyed me, and you ruined my fairytale. God I loved you, I would've done anything for you. I would've never shattered your heart the way that you did mines, but I forgive you Kenneth; if you hurt Jake though, I'll renege on that. You knew he was a slut bucket from the beginning, friend or no friend, the genital of a whore always has the last word."

Kenneth laughs and pulls her into his arms.

"You are still funny as hell, I really miss you Zaya."

"Are you going to go back in and see about your son?"

He takes a long sigh and shakes his head at the sky.

"Yea, let's go back in there."

Zaya detected a little jealousy when Nathaniel asked her about her and Kenneth's conversation outside the hospital, she smiled and teased his bottom lip with a strawberry before feeding it to him.

"I just told him that using Jake as a punching bag wasn't going to change the fact that Kari's not his son. He asked me to forgive him for what he did to me and I said that I do but I will take my forgiveness back if he hurts Jake. Kenneth needs to understand that what goes around comes around, period."

"So are you sure that you're over him? I don't need him popping up at my job trying to punch me out like he did his buddy." says Nathaniel.

"Ha ha ha very funny, no Kenneth and I are over, besides I have my eye on someone else."

He leans forward and kisses her on the nose.

"Oh really, do I know him?" he asks.

"You sure do. He's tall, handsome and successful. When he's nice, he can be so damn sexy."

"Damn this dude sounds like a good catch, do I even stand a chance?"

Getting on all fours and closing the gap between them. She plants a soft kiss on his right cheek, then the left. She kisses his chin and whispers against his lips.

"There's only one way to find out isn't it?"

They were barely through Nathaniel's front door before they began ripping each other's clothes off. He damn near ripped her romper in half along with her bra and underwear and then snatches her off of her feet tossing her over his and shoulder. She nibbles on his shoulder blades as he carries her up the stairs into the bedroom. He throws her onto the bed and slowly unbuckles his pants. His boxers and her mouth both drop simultaneously, he is thick and juicy and she wants every inch of him inside of her. She opens her legs inviting him in but he declines by smacking her legs back together. He mounts her and places his penis in between her breast. She flicks her tongue out as if she wants to lick it.

He rolls onto his back bringing her along; grabbing a handful of her hair with both hands he kisses her deeply. She sucks his bottom lip and pulls, he groans meeting her lips for another hungry kiss. She manages to pull away to leave a trail of kisses down his neck and chest, she twirls her tongue inside of his belly button making him quiver. She separates his legs and nibble on his inner thigh. She takes his manhood into both hands and licks it slowly like an ice cream cone. His breathing deepens and his eyes darken with desire as he watches her handle him. She finally takes him into her mouth as much as she could and swallows repeatedly. He throws his head back and bites his lip. She's working him out until he grabs her by the hair and pulls her away. He pushes her backwards and spreads her legs like bird wings. He buries his face in her wetness provoking soft moans to flee her mouth. He sucks her clit like the nipple on a baby's bottle making it swell.

"Are you ready for me baby?" he asks.

"Yessss, I'm so ready."

He lifts himself over her and places the tip of his penis on her vagina, moving it up and down over her clit.

"Please Nate, please give it to me." she begged.

He slides his hands under her and lifts her, pushing her against the head board. She's now slightly sitting up against the head board awaiting him to merge with her. He nudges her left leg to the side and uses his right hand to grip her hair. Never taking his eyes off of her he eases into her gently; the gasp she makes when he penetrates her is like gasoline on a fire, he pushes inside of her with no mercy.

"Nate!" she screams as she's filled up with him.

He attaches his mouth to hers and moves in and out of her slowly allowing her moist canal to adjust to his hefty package.

"Oooo you're so wet and tight, God you feel good Zaya."

Her moans turn him on and he needs to hear them louder. He wants to make her cry out his name. Once she sucked on his bottom lip he knew to send it into over drive. He put her left leg on top of his shoulder and pounds her with every ounce of strength he has.

"Say my name baby, say it."

"NATE! NATE! OH GOD!"

He could feel her tightening around him like a python. She cries out his name one last time before releasing and trembling in his arms.

"FUCK ZAYA! SHIT!" he pulls out and coats her belly with his salty cream.

He pulls her flat onto her back and plops down on the side of her, burying his head in her neck. They lay panting for a few minutes before he lifts up on his elbows and looks down at her.

"I can kiss these lips every day." The beast in him has subsided, he kisses her softer this time.

"And I can look in these beautiful eyes every day. You surprised me though, I would've never guessed that you were such a freak."

"I was thinking the same thing about you. Not many women can handle the size of me but you were like a pro with it, you knew what you were doing and I like that."

"Baby you have no idea about Ms. Zaya Ardai Martin, this lady is extremely sex intelligent." she says.

He reaches over on the nightstand and grabs a Kleenex to clean her belly.

"Oh yea? Well let's see how good you are." He takes Zaya hand and guides it to his penis.

"You want to go again already?!"

He licks her chin and slides his index and middle finger inside of her.

"Baby you have no idea about Mr. Nathaniel Elijah Thompson, I'm always ready for seconds and according to the wetness and throbbing against my fingers, and you are too." he says.

He kisses her while he jams his fingers in and out of her, and she arches her back and moans. He ate her out as he fingered her leading her to vibrate and cream all over his mouth.

"Forgiveness is the final form of love."~ Reinhold Niebuhr

~Gail~

She hands one of her favorite clients a glass of water then sits across from him. She's so proud of him, he's come a long way from when he first walked into her office. In their first session she discovered that he was a womanizer who blamed women for their own broken hearts. He didn't feel like he was responsible for any pain that he'd brought to any of them. Yep she had her work cut out for her but with patience, love and understanding she found a way to penetrate that tough exterior and get to the root of him. What she found was a grown child yearning for something that he's never had... love.

"Your energy is calmer Nathaniel, your face is more relaxed and instead of insulting my secretary you kissed her instead. Anything you would like to share with me in our final session?"

"Actually I do! Until I met you I hated women, I saw no use for them other than for sexual acts. I never wanted to marry a woman or have children with one because I wanted no ties to them, Zaya makes me want those things. She's so strong and sweet, smart and funny, nurturing and patient. I've never experienced anyone like her in my life and I have you to thank for it." He smiles and nods at Gail.

"This is the second time I've ever seen you smile. Nathaniel and Zaya sitting in a tree, K.I.S.S.I.N.G!"

"Gail you need to stop, anyway, Zaya and I went to see Rachel." he says.

"Really, how was that for you?" She watches the smile slowly leave his face and a bit of sadness mixed with anger appear in his eyes.

"When I laid eyes on her I immediately felt like a little boy again. I was scared and angry at the same time, I wanted to call her mama but I didn't want to set her off, which is silly because she has Alzheimer's. She noticed the animosity in my eyes so she asked me was she a bad mother and I told her that she was the worst mother that a child could ever have." Nathaniel says.

"Oh my, and what was her response?" Gail asked.

"Well dad thought I was out of line but all I did was answer her question. I was about to leave when she stopped me and asked me to elaborate, so I did." he replies.

"Do you mind sharing exactly what happened with me?"

He ran through the entire scenario. He told Gail how he let all of his anger and pain come flowing out after she asked him what it was that she did for him to hate her. He reminded Rachel of some of the cruel things she subjected him to as a child, hearing those things hurt her but he didn't care. He's waited for years to make her feel the same way she used to make him feel... like nothing.

"She apologized to me even though she doesn't remember any of it. She said that she wishes that she hadn't done those things."

"How do you feel about her apologizing and having remorse for what she's put you through?" Gail ask.

"I don't know I still haven't processed it all, I'm just glad that Zaya was there with me." he says.

"It must have felt great to have someone there to genuinely support you." she says.

"Yea it did; besides my father, no one has ever offered or given me anything without wanting something in return."

"Ah, there goes that smile again. I must ask how you two are getting along."

He flashes a Colgate smile and starts to blush.

"We're getting along great, I'm really enjoying the time we're spending together, and she's a wonderful woman. We're taking it slow because we both have some issues that we still want to iron out before we become an item. We don't want to bring any baggage into our relationship."

"That's very mature of you both. Well Nathaniel that concludes our session, it's been a pleasure talking to you, I'm sure this won't be the last time I'll be seeing you."

"No it won't and thank you Gail, for everything." He smiles and gives her a wink before he closes the door behind him.

He walks over to Zaya's desk to confirm their dinner plans, kisses her and assures her that he's going to call her after he performs his final surgery for the day.

Zaya burst into Gail's office with one eyebrow raised and her hands on her hips.

"Um excuse me, my man was smiling a little too hard when he left your office, what were you two doing in here?"

"Girl bye nobody wants Nathaniel's fine successful ass! I was going to speak with you last but since you're in here have a seat."

Zaya made sure no one was in the waiting area before closing the door behind her.

"Gail you act like you're not going to see me outside of here, you are so dramatic!" says Zaya.

"Please look at the pot calling the kettle black Miss Fire starter!"

The laughed simultaneously.

"I know what you want to talk about, you want to know about me and Nathaniel. You are so nosy."

"I'm a therapist, I'm paid to be nosy. So are you still mad at me for sending you out on a date with him?"

"I was at first until he made me cum like a busted fire hydrant. Gail that thing is long and meaty and he hit spots in me that I didn't even know was in there! Girl he had me hitting octaves higher than Mariah Carey." says Zaya.

"Whew that's what I'm talking about! No wonder he was cheesing from ear to ear whenever we brought up your name, you must have put it on him. What I'd really like to know is how was it talking to Kenneth again, did old feelings come back or what?" asked Gail.

"How do you know about that? Nathaniel must have told you, any who, I felt weird seeing him after all this time. I really felt like I needed to get some things off my chest to him and her, and Gail that broad looked like a walking STD, I'm not lying! But I'm glad that I got the chance to tell him how he made me feel doing what he did. I'm also glad that he was man enough to apologize. I feel relieved, now all of that is behind me." Zaya says.

"I'm glad to hear that. You know Zaya, it has been such a pleasure working with you and being friends with you. Your loyalty and love means the world to me and Nathaniel is so lucky to have a woman like you by his side."

"Gail stop, you're always trying to make somebody cry. Let me go, someone's ringing the doorbell." Zaya says as she gives her friend a hug.

Zaya steps into the sitting area to see Morgan standing at the door with her hands on her hips.

"Damn how many times do I have to ring the bell to get up in this joint?!" says Morgan.

"Hey to you too, what's going on girlie? You look all bush tailed and bright eyed today." says Zaya.

"Nothing much, just trying to get my salon back together after what happened. Hey thanks again Zaya for checking on me and everything, I appreciate the love."

"No problem, anytime, Gail's waiting for you in her office."

"When Raven gets here can you send him back? We want to do our session together." asked Morgan.

Morgan knocks, "Knock, knock, hi it's me Morgan."

"Hey Morgan come on in darling, how are you feeling?"

"I'm getting better by the day. You know I go to court in a couple of weeks about the incident, I really don't want to but I know Tim needs to pay for what he tried to do to me. I just hope it hasn't been anyone else he's done this to." answers Morgan.

"Yes he most definitely should answer for his actions, I'm just glad Raven was able to stop him before things went any further." says Gail.

"Yea me too, because of his heroism the International Tennis Federation has lifted his suspension, now he can compete in tournaments again."

The door swings open and in walks her favorite client with a huge smile on his face.

"Gee Gee what's up?!"

"Hello Raven how are you friend?" Gail asked.

"I have the most beautiful woman in the world waking up next to me every morning so I'm great!" He bends down and kisses Morgan.

They kiss for quite some time making Gail blush herself, she had to clear her throat to get their attention.

"So I see the two of you decided to have your last session together, how cute."

"Yea we wanted to thank you for dealing with our crap and bringing us together." Morgan says.

"Well you guys are more than welcome. I'm so proud of you both, you've come a long way from where you were, and especially you Raven." Gail says.

"Yep the playa in me has been laid to rest. All of the women I had staying at my home have been relieved of their duties. I have who I want and she's all the woman that I need." he says.

"Aw babe that's so sweet, give me some kisses." Morgan starts tonguing Raven down causing Gail to roll her eyes.

"Okay you two that's enough, gosh get a room!"

"Hater!" yells Raven.

"Yea y'all are all cute and everything but I need to know this, Morgan have you made peace with Quentin yet? Have you visited his grave and told him how you felt?" asked Gail.

"Gail I don't need to tell him any...." Morgan is cut off by Gail.

"Yes you do Morgan. I care about you but I also care about Raven and I don't want you hurting him because you haven't faced your demon, that wouldn't be fair to him or to yourself. I mean Raven shut that door in his life and bolted it up, he did it violently but at least he's moved past the hurt, it's your turn now."

"Aye Gail, he deserved to catch a few to the face and love bug she's right, you should get it all out of your system before we take this any further." says Raven.

"What the hell? When did you and Gail start agreeing with one another? Okay okay I'll do it, but under one condition," she turns her body to face Raven, "Only if you come with me, I don't want to go through this alone."

He kisses her on the nose and pulls her into his arms.

"Of course I will baby." he responds.

"You two are too damn cute for me, y'all are worse than Zaya and Nathaniel." says Gail.

"Well Gee Gee we must be going we have plans for the Sybaris tonight, we still haven't packed our overnight bags. It's been real as usual." He leans forward and kisses Gail on the cheek

"Talk to you later Gail and get some rest you look beat. Call me if you need anything." Morgan says.

"I will you two have a good time, make love not babies okay? Talk to you guys later." Gail hugs Morgan and walks her to the door.

Gail saw her last few clients for the day, shedding some tears with her good-byes. Today was the last day that she would be a listening ear and shoulder to lean on to so many people. The movers were coming the next day to move out all of the furniture in the office. She knows that it's not going to hit her until she sees her office empty.

Raven notices that Morgan is extremely quiet on the ride home. He knows what's on her mind, he was just waiting for her to say something. She turns to look at him and softly speaks.

"I'm ready to talk to him, I'm ready to put this behind me."

"Put the address into the GPS and we'll go right now." he says.

She enters the destination into the GPS and leans on his shoulder. Lord knows she was going to need it.

They make it to the cemetery just when they were closing the gates for the day.

"Wait! Wait a minute! Could I please see someone? It will only take a minute?" Morgan asked.

The grounds worker with orange hair looks Raven up and down and licks her crusty bleeding lips. She attempts to push her saggy breast up but they just fell right back to the side, so she raised her overall pants leg revealing her hairy calf.

"Sure you can, if he'll come over to my place for dinner." She smiles displaying all three of her candy corn colored teeth.

Raven clutches his stomach and pretends to throw up in his mouth.

"Now lady you didn't have to show me that, you could've just smirked. Standing there looking like a rotten jack-o-lantern get the hell on!" yells Raven.

"Well we close in fifteen minutes so that means you have five minutes, hurry up or sleep with the dead tonight!" she rolls her eyes at Morgan and flicks her tongue out at Raven.

"Ugh just nasty! Go do some work or something!" he says.

It didn't take them long before they came across Quentin's grave; Morgan sat down slowly and lowered her head.

"Hello Quentin long time no see; I haven't seen you since the day I buried you. Well I know you're probably wondering why I'm here after all of this time and there is a reason. I'm ready to cleanse myself of you Quentin; it's time to let you go. I've messed up with some really good men because I was hanging on to what we had and I refuse to lose another one. His name is Raven and he's great. He doesn't treat me like you use to, when he touches me it's with love and respect not with anger and aggression. He actually wants to get to know me, while you on the other hand only were worried about controlling me. Yes, the vacations and the gifts were great but I hated the way that I earned those things. When you smiled that's all I received was your pearly whites but when you frowned, I received punches, slaps, kicks and body slams; soon after the gifts and the trips came. I don't know why I've been holding on to you like you were the idea man because you

weren't, and to think I was about to marry
you. Well Quentin my idea of love was
completely distorted and Gail and Raven
helped me straighten it out."

"You have two minutes left and I'm
closing the gates!" yelled the ground worker.

Morgan stood up and dusted her bottom.

"Well Quentin that's all I had to say...
needed to say. I hope that you are at peace
wherever you are because I am, good-bye."
She reaches for Raven's hand and leads them
out the cemetery.

"Baby are you okay, how you feel?"
asked Raven.

She turns and looks at him with tears in her
eyes.

"I feel free... I feel so damn free."

One year later...

"Who has never tasted bitter does not know what is sweet."~ German Proverb

~Raven~

"I would like to propose a toast; to Gail, the doctors said that you only had six months to one year to live but here you are sitting before us just as beautiful as ever. No doctor can say when we transcend, that's up to the one and only Almighty God, cheers to Gail living and being a part of our lives!" Raven clinks his wine glass with the other party goers.

"Thank you Raven, I love and appreciate you all. Now let's eat and party!" Gail says.

Zaya and Morgan cooked up Gail's favorite dishes and made a playlist of her favorite songs for the party. They danced, played games and told the stories of how they all met Gail. She was happy, they all were. Everything seemed so perfect at the moment and that's all a person can ever really live for is the moment. She was dancing with Nathaniel when a sharp pain shot through her abdomen making her buckle over in agony.

"Gail, Gail are you alright?" asked Nathaniel.

"Yea I'm okay, I just need to sit down for a little while." Gail hasn't told any of them how she's been ill every day for the past three weeks. Everyone has just been so happy with the way their lives were going that she didn't want to worry them with how horrible she's been feeling.

"Here sit in this chair, I'll go get you a glass of water."

"Thank you Nate."

Nathaniel was walking back with the water when the doorbell rang.

"Hello I'm here to see Gail and Gillian please, and might I say you look scrumptious!"

Nathaniel looks the stranger on the other side of the door up and down before calling for Gail.

"Dude please! Gail, someone's here to see you!"

She sees Monroe step inside and instantaneously drops her head, she is not in the mood for his foolishness at the moment.

"Hey Gail happy one year of survival I guess, isn't that why they've thrown you this party? Girl you look just as skinny as me, but for different reasons I suppose, where's mama?"

Without waiting for an answer to his question, Monroe walks into the kitchen calling for his mother.

"Nathaniel, meet my little brother Monroe."

"Can I punch him Gail?"

"Not if Raven beats you to it. Oh this is bad; this is so bad." She downs the glass of water in one big gulp.

"Are you going to be okay?" Nathaniel asked.

"Yea I'll be fine, go check and make sure Raven doesn't have Monroe in a chokehold. I'll be right here when you get back." she says.

Nathaniel checks all of the rooms on the first level and didn't see Raven anywhere so he tries upstairs. He finds Raven sitting on Morgan's bed staring at a black box in his hands.

"What's up Rave, why are you up here and not downstairs enjoying the party?" asked Nathaniel.

Raven shakes his head and hands Nathaniel the black box. Nathaniel opens the box and in it sits a diamond ring encircled by a double row of bead-set diamonds.

"Damn! I've never seen so many diamonds in my life! How many carats is this?"

"One point five, it cost twenty-eight thousand dollars. You think she'll like it?" asked Raven.

"Shit she better, this ring is blinding my eyes. So you plan on asking her soon?"

"Tonight, I'm going to ask her tonight while everyone is here. God I hope she says yes."

"She will, come on let's go back downstairs." says Nathaniel.

The fellas walk downstairs and find Monroe dropping it like it's hot to Ludacris's 'How Low Can You Go.'

"Nate who in the hell is that?!" questions Raven.

"Gail's younger brother Monroe. She told me to keep an eye on you to make sure you don't put him in a chokehold." says Nathaniel.

"Is dude making it clap? Oh hell naw! He's good, as long as he don't get too close."

Raven searches for Morgan and Nathaniel goes to check on Gail, he discovers her with her head down on the table holding her stomach.

"Come on Gail you need to lay down, let me help you upstairs." Nathaniel helps Gail up and allows her to lean on him for support. They were almost at the stairs when they heard Raven call out to them.

"Can I have everyone in the living room please, I have something I would like to say!" yells Raven.

Raven pulls out a chair Morgan to sit down in, he laughs at the confused look on her and everyone else face.

Nathaniel helps Gail sit down and pulls a chair next to hers so he can physically support her.

"Okay is everyone here? Yea? Okay good. I called you all in here so you could be a part of this special moment." He turns to Morgan and runs his fingers through her hair,

"Baby I know that we've only been together for under a year but I love you, I'm in love with you and I've changed so much because of you; you've made me into a better man and I know it's only going to get better in time. You are beautiful, intelligent, funny, strong and loving; I wouldn't trade you in for anything in the world. Morgan baby I wanna spend the rest of my life with you, I wanna wake up and go to sleep with you by my side every single day. I really need you in my life." He opens the box and gets down on one knee, every woman in the room gasped for air.

"Morgan Alicia Cloud, will you please do me the honor of being my wife?"

"Oh my god yes! Yes, baby, yes yes yes!" she wraps her arms around him and they kiss.

The entire room erupted in applause, Gail is too tired to get up and hug them but she did shed a few tears for them.

"Gail, Zaya, Mrs. Shannon look! Isn't it beautiful?" Morgan held her hand out wiggling the diamond on her ring finger.

"Aw look at that little diamond."

Everyone spins around and looks at Monroe.

"Little diamond? This ring is almost two carats, what the hell do you mean little diamond?" says Raven.

"What I mean is for you to be a famous athlete I would've expected a bigger rock than that. Hell the ring Chaz picked out for me was twice as big as that one on her finger."

"Excuse me, come again?" Gail was now standing.

"Oh Gail yea he died before he could tell you. He asked me to marry him and I said yes, we were going to do it right after you guys divorce was final."

"Monroe I didn't invite you here to start some shit!" screams Mrs. Shannon.

"Mother pipe down we're just having a conversation." he says.

"Gail please let me lay his ass out." Nathaniel walks up to Monroe.

"Monroe you have five seconds to get the hell up out of my house before I help you." threatens Morgan.

"Chick simmer down, everyone already knows that I'm a whore, it is not a surprise that I sleep my way around town; men love me and I love them. I can't help it if I satisfied

Gail's husband better than she ever could. What can I say, it's a gift. It doesn't make a difference to Gail anyways she's on her way out of here too. They can make up at the crossroads; hey Gail, see you at the crossroads so you won't be loneeelllyyyyy so you won't be loneeeelllyyyyy, see you at the cross...." he never saw it coming and when he did it was too late. Zaya slaps him across the face with a party tray knocking him to the floor.

Monroe shakes his head and wipes the blood from his mouth.

"I'm about to whip this chick's ass!" He jumps up and tries to go after Zaya but his mother and other guest holds him back.

Nathaniel is trying to get to Monroe but Raven and Morgan is holding him back. No one notices Gail loses her balance. She feels light headed and a rush of heat shoots through her body, the cramps in her abdomen intensified and her legs turned into spaghetti, before she knew it everything went black.

"Gail! Gail! Oh my god someone call an ambulance! Gail!" Zaya rushes to Gail's side.

"There is no revenge so complete as forgiveness."~ Josh Billings

~Gail~

Mrs. Shannon rides in the ambulance with Gail and the rest of the crew follows by car. They were all afraid that this was it, that this was the end. They ran behind the paramedics yelling to Gail that everything will be alright. It seemed like they were waiting in the sitting area for forever before they received an update on Gail. Mrs. Shannon came into the room with her husband both with grim looks on their faces.

"What did they say Mrs. Shannon?" asked Zaya.

"She's not doing too well, the doctors don't give her much time left, and they actually don't think she's going to make it through the night." Mrs. Shannon began to cry into her husband's chest.

"Hey Mister and Misses Shannon, how is she doing?" asked Dr. Erickson as he ran into the waiting area.

"Not so well doctor Erickson, there's a low chance she won't make it through the night." says Mr. Shannon.

"If there's anything that I can do, please don't hesitate to ask." says Dr. Erickson.

"Gillian look, here comes the doctor." Mr. Shannon lifted his wife's head from his chest.

"Mister and Misses Shannon you can see her now but briefly, we don't want to disturb her too much; this is a critical time." says the doctor.

"Doctor, can we see her too?" asked Raven.

"I'm sorry, immediate family only."

"Can I see her?"

They turn around to see Monroe with one side of his face looking like Dizzy Gillespie.

"Why is this idiot always popping up all dramatic and shit out of nowhere? I mean is it just me?" asked Nathaniel.

"Monroe why..." Mrs. Shannon is interrupted by her husband.

Mr. Shannon walks over to his son and smacks him down to the floor.

"Your foolery stops here, it stops right here tonight! You have caused so much unnecessary trouble and pain and I'm not having any more of it! You are a disgrace to this family, your reckless behavior will no longer be overlooked. You are a grown ass child that runs around breaking up happy homes, ruining relationships and friends, demeaning your family and yourself. Until you get yourself together I don't want to see you Monroe do you hear me? I don't want a phone call, a text, a visit, an email, a letter, or a damn post card. I don't want to hear from you until you've cleaned yourself up. You will not be seeing Gail so get the hell out of here and go home Monroe."

"Oh so it's like that dad? You can be there for Gail while she's dying but you're not going to be there for me while I'm doing the same. You two has always showed her more love and I see that will never change." says Monroe.

"You've contracted HIV from sleeping around unprotected; you are reckless in every aspect of your life, Gail is not. She got cervical cancer from HPV and she contracted HPV from her husband who was cheating with you. You brought your fate on yourself, Gail did not. She's a victim of an unfortunate circumstance, Monroe YOU ARE the unfortunate circumstance." Mr. Shannon walks away leaving his son on the floor dumbfounded.

Monroe picks himself up and adjusts his clothing.

"I guess you all agree with my father right?"

"It doesn't matter if we agree, what you have going on is between you and God. Nothing any of us thinks makes a difference." answers Morgan.

"Well I hope you go straight to hell with your sick dick ass!" yells Zaya.

"And I wanna beat your ass so it's best that you don't ask me any questions?" says Nathaniel.

Raven points at Nathaniel, "I second that."

"Fuck all of y'all! Y'all don't know me! I'm a good person, I'm just misunderstood. People mistake my realness as being rude but it's not!"

"If you think sleeping with your sister's husband and bragging about it is being real I feel sorry for you. You have destroyed so many people with your foolishness; your parents, Chaz, Gail and more importantly yourself. Knowing everything you've done, how can you wake up every day and look yourself in the mirror and not have an ounce of regret?" says Zaya.

"Whatever I'm out of here." Monroe gave them all the finger then left.

A few minutes after Monroe's dramatic exit, Mister and Misses Shannon came back from seeing Gail.

"They said for everyone to go home and that they will notify Marvin and me if there are any changes. So you guys should go home and get some rest, I'll call you Zaya with whatever updates I receive." said Mrs. Shannon.

Everyone hugs the Shannon's goodbye and head home. The crew makes plans to meet up the next day to return to the hospital regardless of the call they receive from the Shannon's.

Morgan and Raven make it home first because she lives the closest to the hospital. He starts a shower for them to share, walking her into the bathroom he begins undressing her. He's worried about her, she looks exhausted and afraid. He doesn't like the gloominess in her eyes. Raven kisses her softly and lifts her into his arms. As he steps into the shower he presses her back against the wall. She starts to cry and he kisses her tears away one by one.

She looks at him and begs, "Please make love to me Raven."

He complies and eases inside of her. She digs her nails into his back and buries her face in his neck.

"I love you Raven, I love you so much."

He tells her he loves her back and repeats it over and over again until they climaxed and collapsed. After a few minutes he scoops her up and carries her to the bed. He dries her off and tucks her in. He's never loved someone so much in his life and the need to protect her is strong. He can tell that when the time does come, she's going to need him more than ever; and he plans on being there every step of the way.

Nathaniel and Zaya collapsed as soon as they made it into the bedroom. She crawls into his arms and began to weep, he kisses her forehead and rocks her until the tears no longer fall. Once she was fast asleep he took off their clothes and snuggled up next to her. He wanted to be right next to her when she awakened in case she needed him. He wanted to always be there whenever she needed him. He really loved her and planned on proving it before it was too late.

> *"Forgiving is not forgetting its letting go of the hurt."~ Kathy*

~Nathaniel & Zaya~

After what happened with Gail Nathaniel decided to go visit his mother. His father and Zaya offered to go with him but he told them that it was something that he needed to do on his own. This time around he was more confident, he wasn't afraid to be in the same room with her anymore.

"Hey Rachel how are you?"

"Hello, who are you?" she asked.

"It's me Nathaniel, your son; I just visited you not too long ago."

"I'm sorry I don't remember, what is your name again?

"Nathaniel, my name is Nathan... listen I just came here to letting you know that I forgive you Rachel, I don't hate you anymore."

"Forgive me, for what? What did I do to you Nicholas?"

"Nathaniel, I'm Nathaniel, Nicholas is my dad and you don't rem... okay Rachel, well I just wanted to say that I'm over the past and I would like to keep visiting you if you'd allow me."

"I don't have many visitors so that would be nice. What's your na...?"

"Nathaniel, my name is Nathaniel Thompson."

"Well Nathaniel if you're my son like you say, why do you call me Rachel, shouldn't you call me mom?"

For a brief second fear shot through his body but just as soon as it came it disappeared.

"Because you never allowed me to call you mom, but that's all in the past. I would like to call you mom if that's okay with you."

She opens her arms and waves for him to come to her, he does and he hugs his mother for the first time in his entire life. It was so overwhelming that he started to cry and to his surprise she squeezed him tighter and kisses him on the head.

"Is this what mother's do, hug their children when they're sad?" she asked.

He looks up at her with weepy eyes and smiles.

"Yea ma, this is what mothers do."

Zaya wants to surprise Nathaniel with a candlelit dinner tonight, so she hits up Whole Foods grocery store to get his favorite; lobster tails and crab legs. She's jamming to her iPod when she's bumped from behind.

"Um excuse you chick."

Zaya turns around to see Crystal, Kenneth's wretched baby's mother.

"No chick, you bumped into me thank you very much."

"Yea whatever, watch where you're going or we're going to have some problems."

"How dare you come at me with attitude when you're the one that stole my man, it was not the other way around. You better watch your mouth before I have a flash back up in this joint and that is not what you want, trust me." Zaya warns.

"Ooo I'm scared, let me take a few steps back. Girl please you are the one that doesn't want it. If you were popping that coochie right I wouldn't have had to come in and do your damn job and satisfy your man. But girl you're not missing anything, Kenneth is lame, now

Jake, Jake has an anaconda for a penis and he knows what to do with every inch of it. Kenneth is pissed about Kari not being his but he knew that boy wasn't his, Kari looks nothing like him and he only has my skin tone. I should've left him alone; he's dumb, you're dumb, you two were perfect for each other." Zaya grabs a handful of Crystal's bad weave and bangs her face against a freezer door. She throws her to the floor and turns the shopping cart over on her, kicks her in the face and runs. She makes it to her car and speeds off. She looks in the rearview mirror and laughs to herself.

"Lord I can't believe I just did that! What has come over me?! That was wrong but she deserved it."

The ringtone she'd set for Gail's mother sounded off. She pulls over and grabs her phone out of her purse nervously answering the call.

"Hello? Hello Mrs. Shannon what's the news?"

"She made it through but barely. They are saying that she's going to remain hospitalized from here on out, it's really down to the wire Zaya."

"We're here for her and you guys, we can take shifts at the hospital so you and Mr. Shannon won't get burned out."

"That's sweet of you baby but I'm not leaving my little girls side, but you're more than welcome to visit her."

"Thank you Mrs. Shannon I'd like that a lot, call me when she's awake will you?" asked Zaya.

"I sure will sweetie, talk to you later."

Nathaniel arrives home to the smell of seafood cooking. The dining room table was a romantic set up for two and Sade's sultry voice was softly singing in the background. He creeps into the kitchen to find his beautiful woman in a red lace bra and panties set with a pair of fire red pumps on. She has her hair curly and pulled to one side, she looks delicious.

"Hey honey, how's your mother doing?" she walks over to him seductively and kisses him.

"She didn't remember me, she kept asking me what my name was."

"Oh baby I'm sorry."

"Oh no it was fine. I told her that I was over the past and that I would like to see her more often that's when she opened her arms and signaled form me to give her a hug."

"And did you?" asked Zaya.

"I did and it felt good, I actually cried like a baby and you know what she said?"

"What?"

"She said is this what mother's do, hug their kids when they cry? And I looked at her and said yea, this is exactly what mothers do. Do you know that, that was the first time ever in my life that my mother has hugged me? She didn't even want me near her when I was a child."

"Well I'm glad all of that is over and done for you, you are too good of man to be weighed down with someone else's mistakes; I'm proud of you."

"Thank you baby, what did you do while I was gone?"

"I went to Whole Foods to get us dinner but then I saw Crystal, Kenneth's baby mother well Jake's baby mother and she started talking shit, so I beat her up and then ran. I had to go to a different Whole Foods which pissed me off."

"Wait, wait a minute, baby you beat her up?"

"Yep she got what she deserved but that's irrelevant. I talked to Gail's mom and she says that she will give me a call when Gail wakes up, you know the pain medicine keeps her drowsy." says Zaya.

"Okay well let's eat and get X-rated before we get that call. I'm horny and starving!"

Nathaniel ate like he hadn't eaten in a month, he didn't wait until she was done with her plate before he scooped her from the table and laid her down on the plush rug in front of the fireplace. He took her undergarments off with his teeth and began exploring her body with his tongue. He pressed his tongue against her clit hard and maneuvered it like a rollercoaster causing her to tremble. Her moans sent him over the edge and he took off his pants and entered her with force. She arches her back and screams at his rough entry, she flashes him a smile letting him know that she enjoys the pain as much as the pleasure. His long short strokes began short and rugged; he's pounding her like the face of a hammer to a nail. He pushes her legs back and bangs her harder until she tightens around him like a blood pressure cuff. Her moans have become quicker and louder, she was almost at her release and so was he.

"Don't cum yet baby wait for me, wait for daddy."

He bent down to kiss her never losing his pace or rhythm, he loves her mouth touching his lips.

"You ready baby? Come on let's go, cum for me, cum for daddy."

They moaned simultaneously when they climaxed. He collapsed on top of her, still inside of her, his breath blowing her hair.

"I love you Zaya, I hope that you'll always be mine."

She crosses her legs along his back and trails her nails from his neck to the middle of his back.

"There's no hope, I love you Nathaniel, and I will always be yours."

> *"Gratitude is the fairest blossom which springs from the soul."~ Henry Ward Beecher*

~Morgan & Raven~

Zaya finally got the call from Mrs. Shannon that they could come to the hospital and see Gail. All of them immediately dropped what they were doing to meet up at the hospital. Raven ending his practice training for a tournament; Nathaniel completed his surgery and ran out still in his scrubs; Morgan was in the middle of curling hair when she handed the curling irons to one of the other stylist to finish and Zaya left an important meeting with her corporate boss to rush to the hospital. Raven and Morgan arrived first and shortly after Zaya and Nathaniel.

"Hey y'all have you seen her yet?" Nathaniel asked.

"Not yet we've been waiting on you two plus the Shannon's haven't come down to get us yet." replies Raven.

"Am I the only one afraid to see her in such a weak state like this? I don't know if I can see her and not cry." says Zaya.

"Zaya we have to be strong for her, we can't break down now. She needs us to keep it together." says Morgan.

"I know Morgan, I'm just so scared."

"We all are Zaya, we all are." Raven says.

"Here comes Mr. Shannon," Nathaniel says.

"Hello Sir, how is she doing?" asked Raven.

"Not too good son, they are giving her another couple of weeks to live." says Mr. Shannon.

"Sir, can we see her?" Zaya asked.

"Sure, get some visitor's passes and let's go up."

The ride in the elevator was quiet; Zaya's distressed, Raven's anxious, Morgan's exhausted, and Nathaniel's overwhelmed with emotions he didn't know that he had. When they enter Gail's room they are appalled at here appearance. She looks brittle and depleted, it is clear the cancer has come down on her hard.

Zaya kisses Gail gently on the forehead and cuffs her frail hand.

"Hey love how are you feeling?"

Gail peeks through fluttering eyelids to focus on a blurry image of Zaya, she smirks and squeezes Zaya's hand.

"Hey Zaya, I'm okay, why do you look so sad, do I look that bad?" Gail says jokingly.

"Oh Gail, I'm so sorry but I can't do this. I just can't see you like this." Zaya gives Gail another kiss on the forehead and walks out in tears with Nathaniel closely following behind.

"Mmm, she's such a cry baby. Hey Rave, how are you friend?" whispers Gail.

"I'll be much better when you get out of here Gee Gee." says Raven.

"Raven look at me, when I leave here a sheet will be pulled over my face and I'll be headed to the morgue. Raven there are five stages of grief, do you know what they are?"

"No Gail I don't." he says.

"Well, let me tell you, it goes as follows: Denial, Anger, Bargaining, Depression and finally Acceptance; you my love are in the first stage, denial. I know you, and I know that when I die you will go through each and every last one of these stages without even realizing it."

"Gail, look at me, I don't care what these doctors say, you aren't going to die do you hear me?" He kisses her on the cheek with tears in his eyes.

"See, denial" she snuggles against him.

Nathaniel walks back in with a distraught Zaya.

"Good y'all are back, I was just telling Raven about the five stages of grief. He's in denial and you Zaya, are more than likely past the denial and anger stage. You are at the bargaining stage; you were probably just asking God that if he'll spare me you'll do something different or change something about yourself. Morgan you're in the depression stage; you've given up on bargaining with God and it's hit you like a ton of bricks that my death is inevitable; it is going to happen rather you want it to or not." Gail studies all of their faces and the hurt displayed on them, she looks at Nathaniel and stares a few seconds before speaking.

"And you Nathaniel, you are the strongest of the four and ironically the most logical and understanding of you all. You understood from day one that what's in God's will cannot be changed; you ran express through all of the stages and settled right at the final one, acceptance. You know that's okay that I have to go, you just want to be there for me until the very end, because I presented you something that your mother never have, I gave you love. Well Nathaniel, I love you too, so very much."

They all broke down and took turns hugging and kissing her. They spent a few more minutes talking and laughing before being kicked out by Mrs. Shannon. Raven waits for the others to leave out before him when he approaches Ms. Shannon.

"Mrs. Shannon while we were all in here talking I was thinking, Morgan and I should have a ceremony in the next week or so. I really want Gail to be there since she is the reason we're even together in the first place. I just couldn't live with myself if she wasn't around to see us get married and I'm sure Morgan feels the same way." says Raven.

"I agree with you, I know a very good wedding planner and caterer. I will contact them as soon as you give me a date." says Mrs. Shannon.

"Let's do it next weekend on Saturday, July sixth at four p.m."

"I'm on it, I'll call you as soon as it's booked."

Raven thanks Gail's mother and races to catch up with the others. He finds them in the parking lot talking by his truck.

"Hey babe, is something wrong?" Morgan asked.

"We're getting married next weekend on July sixth at our house in the backyard."

"Honey what, how we going to plan a wedding in under a week?"

"Morgan do you want Gail there or not? How fair will it be that she misses out on something that wouldn't even have happened if it wasn't for her?"

"He's right Morgan, Gail deserves to be there. I'll help you plan everything." says Zaya.

"Baby Mrs. Shannon says that she knows a good caterer and wedding planner, she's calling them today. Here, take my card, you and Zaya go get dresses and all of that stuff. Me and Nathaniel will get suits for us and Mr. Shannon, find a photographer and the entertainment. We have to make this special not just for us but for Gail." Raven says.

"Ooo and I can work with Mrs. Shannon to invite Gail's colleagues, clients and family." Zaya says.

"And I'll invite all of my staff and clients, everyone will have to RSVP within the next three days, Friday June 28th to be exact." says Morgan.

"Okay everyone knows what they need to do so let's get to it."

Raven, Morgan, Nathaniel and Zaya worked feverishly over the following two days to make the arrangements for this overnight wedding. Mrs. Shannon came through with the event planner and caterer. Nathaniel picked up some suits, a DJ and a photographer. Zaya sent out email and text blast to all of Gail's, Morgan's and Raven's contacts. Morgan found dresses and accessories for her, Zaya and Mrs. Shannon, and Raven cut all of the checks.

Back at the hospital, Mr. Shannon cared for his daughter. It hadn't hit him that he was losing her until she was hospitalized. One of the worst fears of a parent is burying their children, no mother or father ever thinks for one second that they will outlive their children. He locked his fingers in hers and brought her hand to his forehead, weeping he began to pray for her and their family.

"Dad..."

"Yes princess?"

"I'm going to miss you."

"Oh baby girl, I'm going to miss you too."

"I know you are I'm your favorite."

"Yep you are. You know Morgan and Raven are getting married next Saturday just for you. They really want you to see the love and happiness you made possible. I think it's a wonderful act of love that they are doing."

"I love them, I love all of them, and you better believe I will be there. Even if I have to roll up in the wedding in a wheelchair, where is it going to be?" Gail says.

"At Raven's home in his backyard," answers her father.

"Makes sense it's big enough, is mom not here because she's helping the girls?"

"Of course she is, she told me she kind of feels like that it's up to her to look out for them since you can't right now."

"I love that lady."

"And she loves you too, do you need anything sweetie? Water, your pillows fluffed?"

"No thank you Daddy, but you can hand me that notepad and pen over there on the stand."

He retrieves the pen and paper from the stand next to the bed and hands them to her. She struggles for a few seconds with getting a good grip on the pen to write. After concentrating for a minute, she manages to get her shaky writing hand under control then slowly begin to write.

"What are you writing honey?" her father asked.

"I'm writing a goodbye letter to my friends."

Everyone met back at Raven's home to discuss how much progress they've made.

"Okay today is Friday, who's coming and who's not?" Morgan ask Zaya.

"Well out of the three hundred people we invited only one hundred and seventy-five RSVP'd." answers Zaya.

"Well then that's all who's getting up in here. Mrs. Shannon you can call the event planner and to notify the caterer that we're expecting one hundred and seventy-five guests." Says Raven.

"Mrs. Shannon can we go over the list one last time please, the event planner got the flowers, decorations, programs, tables and chairs, gifts for the guests" asked Morgan.

"Check!"

"Suits, ties and shoes for the fellas?"

"Check!"

"Dresses, shoes and accessories for the ladies?"

"Check!"

"Pastor Michaels?"

"That was a hard one because you know Pastors don't marry couples until they have had counseling sessions with them but he's agreed to do It." said Mrs. Shannon.

"Ugh, Thank God! Photographer, DJ and the playlist printed out for the DJ."

"Check! Check! And Check!" says Mrs. Shannon.

"Oh, Rave baby, I have something for you." Morgan hands him a black ring box

He opens it to find a wedding band inside, smiling he kisses her.

"Awe baby you didn't have to, I was going to get one tomorrow, thank you though." He hands Nathaniel the box over his shoulder.

"The best man usually holds on to the ring." Nathaniel said.

Raven pats him on the back, "Exactly."

Raven and Morgan saw everyone out after about another hour of going over everything for the wedding, they were frazzled especially Raven. Morgan watches her future husband fight with his shoelaces, he was too tired to untie them so she did it for him. She undresses him and bathes him. She lays him down and uses some warming oil to give him a full body massage. She works out all of the kinks and knots in his back and shoulders until he's sound asleep.

"I know you're sleeping but I'm going to say this anyway, deep down I know Gail knew we were right for each other before we did. I believe that whole singles mixer was to cover up her true plan which was to get you and me and Zaya and Nate to fall in love. At first I was furious with her but then you came for me, you saved my life and I knew that you were the man I was going to spend the rest of my life with. This may sound crazy but I think if Gail would have never gotten sick, she would've never wanted so desperately to lead us into love. Well I'm glad that she did, I can't really imagine life without you. I love you Raven Rahkel Robinson; and I can't wait until I'm your wife." She kisses him on the temple and rolls over to go to sleep.

"I love you too baby and I agree, it was all a plan to get us all together."

"What the hell, I thought you were sleep?!"

"I am now, good night."

She whacks him with a pillow and he catches her hand pulling her over to him. He wraps himself around her and tells her that he loves her until he falls asleep.

"Love is the master key that opens the gates of happiness."~ Oliver Wendell Holmes

~The Ceremony~

The backyard looked amazing; the lawn is a beautiful bright green, the flowers beds and floral urns match the turquoise, purple and white wedding colors. Bows and ribbons are hanging from the trees and fences, the wedding planner decorated the arch with Lily's; Morgan's favorite flowers. The aisle area is decorated with scattered flower petals that give off a special ambiance. There were romantic statues and torches on both sides of the arch for an enchanting effect that promotes love and romance.

"Zaya will you please help me with my veil, Mrs. Shannon isn't here with Gail yet?" asked Morgan.

"You know they had to fight the hospital tooth and nail to let Gail leave in her condition. She can't even stay through the reception; they have to take her back after a while." says Zaya.

"How do I look Zaya?" Morgan twirls in the mirror showing off her gown.

"Oh Morgan you look amazing, this dress is fierce girl, I love this crystal train."

"Zaya you look pretty too. Nathaniel is going to see you and want to take you right then and there at the ceremony. You know that you drive him crazy." says Morgan,

"Girl and I might just let him! Okay it's time to go, your dad is waiting for you." Zaya says.

Everyone drew a breath when Morgan stood at the top of the stairs, she looked devastatingly beautiful.

"Mo Mo, you are the most beautiful bride I've ever seen." said Morgan's father.

"Daddy nobody calls me that! But thank you, do me a favor and don't let me fall and crack my face in this dress okay?" Morgan said jokingly.

"I got you." He kisses his daughter on the forehead and walks her to the door leading into the backyard.

Suddenly Monica's 'Angel of Mine' began to play signaling the guest to rise for the entrance of the bride.

"It's time to go Mo Mo." He looks at his daughter and smiles, he takes her hand and they began their walk down the aisle.

At first Morgan didn't see Gail, but as she got closer to the wedding arch she spots her in the second row on the left. She gives her a big smile and blows her a kiss.

As soon as Morgan makes it to the arch Raven takes her into his arms and kisses her. All the guest including Pastor Michaels burst into laughter

at Raven's impulsive reaction to seeing his future wife.

"Hold on their son, let's bless this first and then you can do all of that." says Pastor Michaels.

"I'm sorry Pastor, she just looks so beautiful, I couldn't help it, I love her." explains Raven.

Those words were all that it took to kick off the water works; everyone was teary eyed, even Nathaniel got a little emotional.

Raven recited his vows first then Morgan followed.

"I, Morgan, take you, Raven, to be my friend, my lover, the father of my children and my husband. I will be yours in times of plenty and in times of want, in times of sickness and in times of health, in times of joy and in times of sorrow, in times of failure and in times of triumph. I promise to cherish and respect you, to care and protect you, to comfort and encourage you, and stay with you, for all eternity."

Once Pastor Michaels pronounces them husband and wife, they share a long kiss, and then simultaneously they jumped the broom. As the newlyweds ran down the aisle together, every wedding guest showered them with white rose petals and congratulations.

The wedding planner guides the guest to the other half of the yard for the reception. The wedding goers are seated under a purple tent embellished with amazing centerpieces and lighting. The food set up is buffet style with every table having their choice of ten different wines to choose from. Morgan's father, Gail, Zaya, Nathaniel, and the Shannon's sat on both sides of the bride and groom chairs awaiting the start of the reception.

"Gail we're all so glad that you're here, did you see Morgan's face when she seen you sitting out there? She lit up like a Christmas tree!" says Zaya.

"She looked beautiful, I've never seen a prettier bride." replies Gail.

"Gail you don't look too bad yourself." says Nathaniel.

"You're just getting mushier by the hour, Zaya whatever you're doing to this man, keep it up." says Gail.

Everyone erupts into applause when the DJ announces the entry of the newlyweds. The two of them stroll to their seats smiling from ear to ear, waving and shaking hands along the way. Gail waits until Raven and Morgan take their seats before capturing everyone's attention.

"Excuse me everyone, I would like to say a few words before we begin our feast. Unfortunately, I'm too weak to stand and project my voice to the back of the tent, so I apologize if you struggle to hear or see me... I would like to congratulate Raven and Morgan on following their hearts and making their love official. I met these two at two different times in my life and I knew from the first day we met, they would be a part of my life and I in theirs. Everyone in here knows that Raven is the bad boy of tennis and he stays in time out."

She looks over at him as he tries to hide his face. "Don't cover up your face, you shouldn't be so darn bad. Well he was told by the International Tennis Federation gods that if he didn't seek counseling for his temper, he wouldn't be able to play professional tennis again, and whew, when I say that this man's mind was under lock and key, if Harry Houdini was locked inside Raven's head he wouldn't be able to get out. But I didn't give up; every session I chipped away at him until he became more comfortable and relaxed. Soon I went from Gail to Gee Gee and that's when I knew we were making progress. And I met Morgan here due to the fact that the beautician that I had at the time never showed up to her shop on time for my appointment. I was a guest speaker at this huge conference so I needed my hair styled. So I walked into her shop to get an emergency do and seen something funny but sad. I had seen four different men come up there giving her credit cards, keys to cars and bags filled with name brand accessories. I couldn't believe that I was getting my hair done by a female pimp." Gail gazes left when Morgan begins to cough, "Morgan stop there's nothing wrong with your throat, anyway, we talked until the shopped closed that night and I learned why she was who she was so I offered a free session and the rest is history. I've grown to love you both; not only have you two helped me with my personal crap, but also Zaya and Nathaniel here; you four are the best and I wish all of you, all of the love and happiness in the world. God bless you Morgan and Raven, may you two live happily ever after." Gail lifts her glass signaling the end of her speech and everyone else followed.

"Aw Gail we love you too, I'm mad you put my business out there like that though." Morgan kisses her friend on the cheek.

"Girl please, everyone knows that you were a hot in the ass back then stop it." says Gail.

Zaya and Nathaniel gave toast as well, Nathaniel offered words of encouragement which brought a smile to Gail's face and Zaya was so choked up that they could barely understand what she was saying. The tent was filled with music, laughter and love. Everyone was having a good time, eating, drinking and fraternizing; the DJ brought everyone to the floor when he played J Dash song "Wop". Even though Gail was wheelchair bound she still joined everyone in the fun. Raven and Morgan slow danced to Tamia and Eric Benet's 'Spend My Life With You'.

"Zaya I'm a little parched could you please give me a glass of water?" asked Gail.

"Sure I'll be right back." says Zaya.

Heat and sharp pains rush through Gail's body causing her to double over in discomfort, her breath quickens and her vision becomes blurry. Nathaniel just happens to look back in search of Zaya only to spot Gail with her head down and her arms wrapped around her waist.

"Gail, Gail are you okay, do you need to go back to the hospital?" he asked.

"No, not the hospital, I just need to lie down for a bit that's all." She had already made it up in her mind that she wasn't about to die in a cold hospital room, she didn't deserve that.

He rolls her into the house so she could rest in one of the bedrooms on the first level. He lifts her from the wheelchair and lies her down in the bed.

"Gail I think we should take you back to the hospital you don't look too good, I'm going to get your parents."

"No Nathaniel wait, sit down and talk to me for a second."

"Gail I really think..."

"Please Nathaniel, just for a second."

He can't resist her tired pleading eyes so he gives in and lies next to her.

"Thank you, so when are you proposing to Zaya?" she asked.

He reaches inside of his pocket and pulls out a red suede box.

"I want to ask her tonight before everyone leaves, I didn't want to steal the spotlight from Raven and Morgan that's why I'm waiting to the very end. I hope we have your blessings." he says.

"Of course you do, I think you're going to be an amazing husband to her and an awesome dad to your future children."

"I sure hope so, I really do love her Gail; she's the best thing that has ever happened to me. I spent hours deciding on an engagement ring to present her with. I had to find the perfect ring for the perfect woman. Hell, I even attempted to sit down and write out what I was going to say to her when I got down on one knee, I can't tell you how many sheets of paper I went through, I damn near used an entire spiral notebook. Gail I've never put so much time and effort into anything my entire life. I've always been good in my studies so medical school was a piece of cake for me..."

His voice was becoming a whisper to her, the pain was overwhelming her and she just didn't have it in her anymore to put up a fight. They had intertwined fingers in the midst of him talking and her grip was loosening slowly. She couldn't keep her eyes open any longer and the tears began to flow.

"Nathaniel... I... love you guys... so... much... I love you..."

"We love you too Gail. So do you think I should do it tonight or plan a special day to do it?" He looks down at his hand because her fingers fell away from his. He turned and looks down at her, her face is relaxed and wet from tears.

"Gail can you hear me, you can't go yet, Gail..."

She never answers him. He kisses her forehead and lingers there crying still asking her don't go.

Zaya had been looking for Gail and Nathaniel for the past ten minutes. She asked many of the guests before one of Raven's tennis friends said he'd seen them go into the house. She walked in and saw Gail's wheelchair parked by one of the guests' rooms.

"Hey babe is she sleeping? She asked for a glass of water, I went to get it and she was gone. She's probably exhausted from the day's events, babe?"

He looks up at her with tears in his eyes and shook his head. She rushes to the bed and checks to see if Gail is breathing but she is not.

"Oh my god Gail!" she lies her head on Gail's chest and starts to cry.

Nathaniel reaches over and lifts her head up to look at him.

"You stay here, I'll let them know."

He tries to wipe the tears from his face but they rapidly continue to fall. He steps out into the yard and looks around at everyone celebrating; he is reluctant to walk over to her parents, they look so happy slow dancing and singing to each other.

Mrs. Shannon sees Nathaniel's gloomy expression and approaches him.

"Hey Nate, you've been crying, did Zaya break up with you?" she asked.

He hugs her and breaks down, "I'm so sorry... she's gone."

She pushes away from him, "What? No, where is she? Where's my baby?"

He tells her and she bolts into the house. When she makes it to the room Zaya's already there, kneeled down beside Gail crying on her chest. She runs over and wipes the tears from her daughters face before releasing her own. Soon after Mr. Shannon, Nathaniel, Morgan and Raven ran into the room. all sobbing and holding on to each other in disbelief that the day they absolutely dreaded has finally fell upon them; God had called his angel home.

"Gone; the saddest word in any language."~ Mark Slouka

~Goodbye~

On the way to the burial site the song "Numb" by Sia comes on the radio; Zaya turns it up and sings along.

"I saw you cry today

The pain may fill you..." She looks over at her fiancé and brushes his face with her fingers.

"You know Gail use to listen to this song all of the time when we were at the office and I couldn't stand it. I asked her, 'Why do you play that sad depressing song every single day?' and she said, 'Because it speaks for and to so many of us; listen to the words, you might find yourself or someone else in the midst of them; I know I have.' I never questioned her about it again. Only just the other day did I really listen to the song and she was right, I did find someone within it... I found her." says Zaya.

"I just want to know why she only wanted to be buried and not have a funeral." says Nathaniel.

"That's Gail, trying to eliminate as much grief as she can. She didn't want to take us through all of that, she wanted to make it easier for us." she says.

"Well it's not easy accepting that she's gone." he says.

"I know babe, it might not ever be."

Pastor Michaels waited for everyone to arrive at the burial site so he could offer some words of comfort to Gail's family and friends.

"Today we are gathered together for the graveside service for Doctor Gail Miranda Washington. On behalf of the family, I would like to thank all of you for coming today; everyone bow your heads and let's pray... The Lord is my shepherd: I shall lack nothing. He makes me lay down in green pastures. He leads me beside still waters. He restores my soul. He guides me in the paths of righteousness for his name's sake. Even though I walk through the valley of the shadow of death, I will fear no evil, for you are with me. Your rod and your staff, they comfort me. You prepare a table before me in the presence of my enemies. You anoint my head with oil. My cup runs over. Surely goodness and loving kindness shall follow me all the days of my life, and I will dwell in the house of the Lord forever."

The entire audience recited the shepherd's psalm along with Pastor Michaels, adding a comforting touch to the opening of the service. He touched on how death reminded us of an imperfect world and the shadow that has been casted over humanity because of Adam's sin. He said death also reminded us that life triumphs over death.

"So don't you weep, for everything there is a season, and a time for every matter under heaven; I'm now going to step back and let you focus your attention on Gail's father; Mr. Shannon you may come up now." says Pastor Michaels.

Gail's father stood in front of the crowd with swollen eyes and folded sheets of paper.

"Last week when Gail was in the hospital she says dad I'm going to miss you, and I say I'm going to miss you too; she says I know because I'm your favorite. That was Gail, always trying to make light of a situation. She asked me to hand her the pen and notebook that was on the table in the room; I asked her why and she said that she was going to write a goodbye letter to her friends; so I'm going to read the letter she wrote here today."

"Dear My Loves,

If any of you are reading this letter that means I've transitioned on. Oh how I'm going to miss you all for my own special reasons. I don't want any of you to mourn me; I want you all to live for me. You four have something that I never had the pleasure of experiencing... and that's true love. In case you guys haven't figured it out yet I'll tell you; that whole singles mixer party was a mapped out plan to get you four to date each other. I knew you wouldn't give each other a second look on your own, so I had my mother assist me in getting you four together. Yea I'm sneaky like that; it worked so I'm not ashamed about it; okay enough of that let's talk about Zaya. Zaya a girl couldn't ask for a better best friend; we've been through so much together. You were there for me at the lowest point of my life and it was nothing in the world I could've ever done to pay you back. I knew the first time I met Nathaniel that he was the one for you; you balance him out; you are the yin to his yang. Don't you ever change Zaya for anyone; you are a wonderful person and an amazing woman; Nathaniel should thank his lucky stars for you. Speaking of Nathaniel, I must admit that I wanted to karate chop you when you first walked into my office, but I'm glad that I didn't. After the first five minutes of our session I knew exactly what you needed... pure untainted love. Once I realized that, getting you and Zaya together was at the top of my agenda. You are not only a wonderful pediatric surgeon, but you're an awesome man that has so much love to give and Zaya's heart is big enough to receive it all. Now to my Miss Morgan; girl the talks we've had in my office and your shop were priceless and hopefully never get out to the public. You kept me laughing and on my toes with your wittiness and I don't take no crap attitude. I knew Raven was perfect for you; with your feistiness and his, I knew that you two would fall in love and fast. And Raven... my sweet, sweet Raven, you stole my heart from the beginning. It's no secret that you're my favorite, tell Zaya to stop pouting she already knows this. You put me through so much! I had to go back to my college psychological text books to see how to deal with you because you were off the chain! I never regretted one moment that we spent together. It was my life's mission to get you what you deserved and that was a peace of mind and a mended heart. Now I'm not saying that I'm God, but I know helping people to emotionally heal is my calling. God ordained me to assist people in facing those demons and finding inner peace. I know you're having a hard time accepting my departure and that's okay, that's normal, but don't dwell in that sad place for too long Raven; I want you to live happily with the woman you've been waiting all of your adult life for. She deserves the best of you, don't let my passing interfere with that. I want all four of you to know that I will miss you dearly and I'll be watching from above. Please don't ever forget me, if you do, I'll terrorize your children for generations to come, just joking but not really. I love every single last one of you with every ounce of energy I have left. Be good to yourselves and be good to each other; goodbye my loves, I'll put in a good word for you... I promise."

Love always,

Gail

P.S. ~ Tell Monroe that I still love him despite of it all and that he will always be my little brother no matter what."

Mr. Shannon wipes his eyes and returns to his seat; Raven, Zaya, Morgan and Nathaniel were all crying and smiling at Gail's words. They didn't tell her but they had already figured out that the party was a set up to get them all interested in one another.

One by one everyone at the burial site placed roses on top of Gail's casket, stopping briefly to say a small prayer before she was lowered into the ground. The grounds worker began to lower the casket into the ground but Raven stopped him; he runs his hand along the casket then kisses it. He places his arms on top as if he's hugging her; he tells her that he just can't accept her being gone and he won't.

"Raven, son it's time to go; they have to lower her into the grave honey." says Mrs. Shannon.

"I'm not ready." he says.

"Come here, let's talk." She hooks her arm in his and pulls him away.

"Raven none of us was ready for this day, even though we knew it was only a matter of time, we still weren't ready. You heard what she wrote; she wants you to live for her. Show her that her last good deed wasn't in vain. Prove to her that you can love your wife like she thought you could Raven, make her smile down on you from heaven. We were all being so selfish with her; it didn't matter that she was in pain, it didn't matter that she was suffering, all we cared about was her sticking around for the sake of our own feelings. How fair were we being to her when she cared more about our feelings than her own feelings? I'm telling you, what we have to do is do right by Gail. We have to take what she's taught us and run with it. My baby served her purpose on this earth and what a great purpose it was. You hear me Raven, don't you lose yourself in her demise understand me?" asked Mrs. Shannon.

"Yes I hear you. You know you're a great mom Mrs. Shannon, I can see where Gail got her wisdom from." says Raven.

He walks her to her car and tells her that he will meet her at her home for the repast. He finds his wife sitting on a bench talking with Zaya and Nathaniel; he walks up on the butt of the conversation.

"Zaya I think that's a great idea, we should really look into that." says Morgan.

"Well honey, I've been thinking that I should do for others what Gail has done for us." Zaya says.

Confused Raven sits next to her, "I don't understand what you're saying; break it down for me."

"I'm saying that Gail noticed that we all yearned for the same thing and that was to be loved and in love so she devised a plan to give us the desires of our heart. I think I should do the same for others that were like us... sort of like a match making service." says Zaya.

"She'd be like a Loveologist... a love coach." says Morgan.

"But baby don't you have to study and get certified in loveology?" asked Nathaniel.

"Yes, I've already did the research and found different schools that offer what I need to get certified." Zaya says.

"Zaya has the heart, the patience, the personality; I think this is a good career choice for her." says Nathaniel.

Raven looks at his friend and smiles, "Zaya Martin, the Loveologist, I like it."

They all agreed to pitch in and help Zaya get her practice off the ground once she receive her certification.

"Come on y'all let's go, I know they're waiting for us at the repast." Morgan says.

They were all walking to the car when Zaya turns back one last time.

"I love you too Gail and I promise that all of the good you've done for us and countless others won't go unrecognized; everyone will know who you were... you can believe that." She blows a kiss at Gail's grave and whispers a final goodbye.